A LOUD ROAR
FILLED SPIDER-MAN'S EARS

He shook his head to clear away the annoying thundering that threatened to split his aching skull. His head banged against metal.

The Web-slinger's eyes snapped open.

What the . . . ?

He was upright with his hands chained to his sides and bound to a curving metal surface inside a deep, brightly lighted pit that was alive with clouds of billowing, swirling gas. He was vibrating violently. . . . No, the surface he was chained to was shaking with the fury of powerful pent-up forces.

"Ten. Nine. Eight."

Spidey heard the words faintly through the deafening roar. *A countdown!*

They're getting ready to launch their microwave doo-hickey into orbit!

And guess who made it on to the passenger list at the last minute!

Spider-Man strained against the chains, exerting as much power as he could muster. It wasn't enough.

Maybe these things will give eventually, but the old clock on the wall tells me I'm rapidly running out of any and all eventuallys!

"Two. One. Lift-off!"

A NOVEL BY PAUL KUPPERBERG

MURDER MOON

**Packaged and edited by
Len Wein and Marv Wolfman**

PUBLISHED BY POCKET BOOKS NEW YORK

Another *Original* publication of POCKET BOOKS

POCKET BOOKS, a Simon & Schuster division of
GULF & WESTERN CORPORATION
1230 Avenue of the Americas, New York, N.Y. 10020

ISBN: 0-671-82094-X

First Pocket Book printing November, 1979

10 9 8 7 6 5 4 3 2 1

Trademarks registered in the United States and other countries.

Printed in the U.S.A.

To Ann DeLarye-Gold and Mike Gold
and
their dining room table.

MURDER MOON

Chapter 1

"GAMMA BASE, THIS IS SKY SPY ABLE. We've spotted your bogey, headed due south in Sector Charlie. Over."

The army helicopter swept out of the sky from the southeast, its rotors beating a deafening tattoo in the still, dry air over the New Mexican desert. Before the two men in the military aircraft stretched a seemingly endless expanse of sand, shimmering golden yellow in the glare of the midday sun. For as far as they could see there was nothing but the sand, bleak and foreboding and devoid of even the slightest sign of civilization, of life—save for the lone figure that trudged wearily through the stifling heat far below the speeding chopper!

"*Roger, Sky Spy Able. Can you confirm bogey as Target Green? Over.*"

Captain William Martin squinted through his green-tinted sunglasses at the solitary figure moving steadily into the distance. "Can't be sure from here, Gamma Base," he said into his microphone. "Hold while I take her down for a better look. Over."

"We read you, Sky Spy Able. We're holding on Alert Minus One."

Martin pushed down on the control stick and sent the chopper into a sharp descent toward the barren landscape. "Think it's him, Max?" he shouted to his companion over the din of the whirling rotor blades.

"Let you know in a sec, Cap'n," Lieutenant Max Wilson shouted back. He raised his binoculars and peered through them, focusing on the figure below. "Well, it's a guy, all right," Wilson muttered. "Big fella, too. And he's—he's—"

"He's what?"

". . . green?"

Martin's head jerked up in surprise and his hand tightened on the throttle. "Green? You *sure*, Max?" he asked, his voice tense with expectation.

Wilson shook his head in uncertainty. "Hard to say, sir, what with the heat distortion and . . . *holy cow!*"

The big man had stopped dead in his tracks as the helicopter passed over his head. He was a giant of a man, clad in the tattered remains of a pair of purple trousers, fully seven feet tall, with thick, rippling sinews. As he stared up at the aircraft, his eyes were dull and brutish beneath a protruding brow.

And his skin was a deep emerald green.

The Incredible Hulk's lips curled into a savage snarl of rage at the copter. Though his thoughts were muddled, confused, the sight above sparked a hint of recognition in his bestial mind. He dimly remembered that thing in the sky, or things just like it, and he remembered it with hatred. Many times in the past they had come after him when he desired nothing more than to be left in peace.

But always they attacked him.

Always they hounded him.

"No!" he roared. "Everywhere Hulk goes puny men follow."

The Hulk flexed his thickly muscled legs and propelled himself into the sky toward the speeding aircraft as effortlessly as a normal man might step up onto a curb.

"But no more! Hulk will smash!"

Lt. Wilson saw the green-hued man-monster grow in his field of vision through his binoculars. He whipped them away from his eyes and stared at the approaching figure in awe. It just wasn't possible!

"Come in, Gamma Base," he shouted hoarsely into the mike. "We confirm bogey in Sector Charlie *is* Target Green! Repeat, we *have* the Hulk in . . ."

"You mean he's got *us*," Martin cried.

The helicopter shuddered, its nose dipping suddenly toward the ground a hundred yards below as the Hulk's massive hands wrapped around the craft's landing gear. "Jeez," Martin hissed through clenched teeth. "H-he's pulling us down, Gamma Base. I can't stay aloft!" The army pilot wrestled frantically with the controls, but it was a fight he could not hope to win. All he could do was watch in wide-eyed terror as the ground seemed to rush up toward the service ship, dragged down by the Hulk's ponderous weight.

"We copy, Sky Spy. We have gone to Alert Zero. Reinforcements are on their way. Over."

With a spine-wrenching jolt, the Hulk landed, holding the copter above his head. The machine struggled against the green giant's hold, its rotors beating uselessly against the air.

"Stupid men try to stop Hulk with stupid machines," the man-brute growled.

Martin and Wilson clawed desperately at the buckles of their safety harnesses and released them. They leaped from the cockpit to the relative safety of the burning sand. Wilson grunted and scrambled to his feet. With a trembling hand, he pulled the pistol from the holster at his side and leveled it at the monstrous being that held the helicopter like a small, frightened bird.

"Cap'n . . . ?"

Bill Martin rose slowly to one knee and gestured at the other man. "Put that damned thing away, Wilson!" he ordered harshly. "You can't hurt him with it but you *can* make him madder'n hell."

The Hulk stared with emerald eyes full of rage at the man with the gun. "Puny man," he grunted. "Puny man wants to hurt Hulk with toys, but Hulk cannot be hurt by you!"

Casually, the man-monster tipped the helicopter to the sand, then dashed it against the ground like a toy. The still-whirling rotors dug into the sand with a loud screeching before breaking off and flying through the air. The Hulk turned to face Wilson with the twisted remains of the landing gear gripped like a club in his mighty green fist. With a snarl, he advanced toward the frightened army officer.

Wilson blanched and screamed incoherently in fear. His finger tightened spasmodically on the trigger.

Bang! Bang!

The green Goliath growled in annoyance as the bullets bounced harmlessly off his thick, virtually invulnerable hide.

"Now it is Hulk's turn, little man!"

Suddenly, the desert calm was shattered by the distant scream of approaching sirens and the steady, loud chopping of propellers in the sky overhead. Like an army of invading locusts, the closely grouped horde of approaching helicopters darkened the distant sky. The speeding military vehicles on the ground kicked up a billowing cloud of sand in their wake.

The Hulk growled menacingly.

Wilson backed away from the man-brute, his breath leaving his lungs in a shuddering sigh of relief. The cavalry had arrived!

His bestial mind quickly forgot about the two army men in the face of this newer, more potent foe, and the big green man absently brushed Wilson aside. The lieutenant sprawled in the sand several yards from the Hulk, bruised, but otherwise uninjured.

"Go away!" the Hulk roared to the skies.

But they kept on coming.

Captain Martin rushed to his comrade's side. "You all right?" he whispered quickly.

Wilson shook his head. "I'm still breathing," he said.

"Good." Martin yanked the other man to his feet. "If you want to *keep* breathing, though, we'd better get the hell out of the area. 'Cause any second now, those guys are going to start lobbing everything they've got at the Hulk and I sure as hell don't want to be caught in the middle of *that* shooting match!

"C'mon!"

All the emerald-skinned mammoth's attention was riveted on the approaching helicopters. He did not notice the two men scrambling for safety.

The lead helicopter swooped over the Hulk.

"Dr. Banner!" A voice was calling to him from the chopper's PA system. "We do not wish to harm you, Dr. Banner. Repeat, we will *not* hurt you if you surrender to us now."

"Bah! Don't talk of puny Banner to Hulk! The Hulk is not puny Banner, Hulk is Hulk!" the behemoth roared, shaking his emerald fist threateningly at the heavens.

"I ask you one more time, Dr. Banner! Surrender yourself to one of our helicopters and we will not hurt you!"

With a savage snarl of defiance, the green Goliath whirled and loped over to Martin's downed chopper. He dug his thick, powerful fingers into the twisted metal body and with scarcely a sign of effort, hefted it above his head.

"Hulk said Banner is *gone* and Hulk knows!" he bellowed. "Because Hulk is the strongest one there is!"

With a grunt, he heaved the wreckage at the hov-

ering chopper. The pilot shouted in surprise and tried
to wheel his craft out of the speeding missile's path.
But the Hulk's aim was true and, with a scream of
tearing metal, the wreckage sheared the tail section
from the copter.

The Hulk's emerald lips curled with a growl of
satisfaction as the damaged aircraft, struggling to remain airborne, spun like a wounded bird to land with
a crash in the sand.

The clank of machinery caught the green mammoth's attention next and he turned to see a huge,
specially modified military tank wheeling steadily toward him. The mounted cannon swiveled on the
tank's turret and took aim at the man-brute.

"When will stupid men learn to leave Hulk alone?"
he yelled angrily at the steel-blue metal creature. It
continued rolling on.

The tank fired, belching flame and smoke from the
cannon, and the Hulk leaped. The missile whizzed by
him and, a second later, the great green man landed
heavily atop the tank.

"Hulk will teach puny men," he grumbled. He
crouched and grasped the cannon in his emerald
hands. He tugged it toward him, wrenching it free of
its mooring.

Then the man-brute leaped to the ground, swinging
the heavy cannon like a massive baseball bat.

Thwoom!

The big tank tipped, one side lifting off the ground
from the force of the mighty blow. It hung balanced
on one tread and then began spinning in a circle like
a child's toy before toppling over on its side.

The man-monster turned to face two more similarly
modified tanks rumbling toward him across the desert.

"Men still want to fight Hulk, eh?"

In reply, both cannons fired simultaneously. The
shells hissed through the air and thudded into the
sand on either side of the Hulk. With a loud *whoosh*,
the shells burst open, releasing their noxious cargoes
of gas into the air. The fumes swirled around the Hulk,

the golden cloud enveloping him as if attracted to him
in some mysterious way.

The man-monster swung his muscular arms wildly
before him, trying to disperse the gaseous cloud that
was already beginning to sap his prodigious strength.
He remembered clouds like this from other times,
other places. And though his primitive mind was
veiled by a foggy haze of rage and hate, he knew one
thing for certain:

"Hulk must fight cloud!"

Like a maddened bull, the green-skinned behemoth
charged from the gas, swiping angrily at the wispy
tendrils that clung to and followed his giant form. The
first thing he saw through stinging eyes was another
one of the tanks.

With an unintelligible roar of rage, he leaped toward it. He landed directly in front of the rolling tank
and, planting his feet firmly in the sand, threw his
weight against it. The armored machine shuddered
and the driver gunned the engine. The treads spun
wildly in the sand, digging in as the mighty Hulk
strained against the tank. Then, his muscles knotting
beneath his glistening, emerald skin, the man-brute
forced the tank slowly back. Gears screamed in protest as the driver urged his vehicle forward to roll over
the superhuman obstacle, but in this meeting of ir-
resistible force and immovable object, the object won.

Oily smoke billowed from the tank's engine as the
Hulk shoved it backward across the sand toward the
remaining tank.

Klaang!

Both machines buckled under the violent impact.
And, though the damage to the second tank was not
great, the other tank wedged tightly beneath it effec-
tively immobilized it.

The Hulk stepped back and surveyed his handiwork with a savage snarl of satisfaction. He looked
about. The helicopters had retreated, maintaining as
much distance and altitude as was possible while still
keeping the emerald colossus in sight. But there was

something else up there, beyond the hovering choppers—several tiny dots that grew larger even as the
Hulk watched.

And then the sky was alive with the rapidly approaching whine of speeding jet fighters.

They roared out of the east, a quartet of rocketing
fighter planes flying in tight formation. They zoomed
in low, overflying the Hulk and then climbing back
into the sky. Still in formation, they executed a smart
180-degree turn and headed back in toward their target.

"More stupid men in metal birds!" the brute
grunted. "They think they are safe from Hulk way
up in sky."

He bounded over to where he had dropped the dislodged cannon and hefted it in his jade hands. Whirling, he tossed it into the air like a javelin.

"But stupid men are wrong!"

Like a missile, the heavy cannon streaked skyward.
It tore through the wing of the fighter on the right
wing of the formation before the astonished pilot saw
what it was that had hit him. Suddenly, though, he
had lost control of his fighter and was spiraling down
toward the ground. He ejected just seconds before his
plane exploded against the desert floor in a billowing
mushroom cloud of flame and black smoke.

The other fighters veered off, breaking formation.

They formed a line and, one by one, passed over
the green Goliath as, one by one, they fired small
missiles from beneath their wings.

The missiles seemed to take on a life of their own
as they streaked toward the Hulk. Instead of striking,
they buzzed about the man-monster like a swarm of
mosquitoes, circling the Hulk as if seeking an opportunity to strike.

They were drones, computerized slave mechanisms
guided via radio from a bunker more than a dozen
miles away. Miniaturized cameras in the missiles'
noses allowed their operators to home in easily on the
large green man. And, when they did, the three oper-

ators gave three simultaneous radio commands to their flying charges.

Fwhit!

Shiny steel cables, no more than an inch thick, shot from the missiles. Guided by computerized sensors, the cables snaked toward the Hulk. They slithered from the missiles and whipped around him.

Growling in annoyance, the Hulk flailed his massive arms at the silvery tentacles. His hand wrapped around one cable, but before he could put it out of commission, a second cable wound its way around his neck.

The jade giant's hands flashed to his throat, desperately trying to dig his fingers under the cable and tear it away. But the steel snake's hold was firm and, before the man-brute realized it was happening, the others were winding their way around his massive body. Within seconds, the cables had enveloped him like a cocoon woven of solid-steel strands.

He struggled in the stifling bonds, but with each moment the trap thickened and tightened around him. Cautiously, the choppers moved in to take a closer look, certain now that the great green menace was at last subdued. After all, they reasoned, those cables were made of a new, nearly indestructible alloy developed for Gamma Base by Stark Industries. Nothing alive, they were told during the course of their briefing, could snap them.

Not even the Incredible Hulk.

The man-creature snarled savagely. He was securely trussed up from neck to knees, his mighty arms pinned awkwardly to his chest.

"Let Hulk go or Hulk will make puny men sorry!" he roared.

The Hulk gritted his teeth, growling. They would not release him, he knew. Every time they caught him in their traps they took him away and put him in a cage.

And the Hulk hated cages.

Even more, the Hulk hated being tied up like a helpless weakling, like that puny Banner!

And what the Hulk hated, the Hulk smashed!

His massive muscles flexed under the metallic cocoon. They bulged like thick, knotted ropes under his skin, exerting the full power of the Hulk's Gamma radiation–mutated strength against his bonds. Beads of perspiration stood out like tiny, shimmering emeralds on his forehead as he strained, his anger growing greater with each passing moment of frustration.

And as the jade-hued giant's anger increased, so did his strength!

With a sharp snap, the cables began to break. With a mighty roar, he threw the shattered strands aside.

"Hulk has had enough of puny men and machines," he growled to the men in the hovering choppers.

He leaped into the air, flying toward the nearest helicopter with his arms stretched out before him like a battering ram. The pilot saw the green mammoth flying toward the cockpit in time to duck, for, in the next instant, the great, green projectile smashed through the transparent bubble and continued skyward. The pilot took one look at his shattered controls and bailed out.

The Hulk continued on, twisting his body in midflight to swerve toward the second copter. This time, though, the pilot realized it was impossible to avoid a head-on collision with the green giant. He pulled free of his safety harness, checked his parachute and leaped from the aircraft. Within seconds, that aircraft was reduced to falling debris by the Hulk's emerald fists.

With ground-shaking impact, the colossus landed in the now flaming debris-littered desert. He snarled once at the men scattered about him and jumped into the air, this time his powerful leg muscles propelling him miles through the sky.

Within seconds, the great jade giant was gone from view.

Captain Bill Martin squinted into the sun after the receding figure. "I'll be damned . . ." he muttered, looking stunned.

"You said it, Cap'n!" Lieutenant Max Wilson breathed. "Did you see the way that monster snapped those cables like they were string!"

"Yeah. Jeez, I hope the next time he shows up, he doesn't do it *here!*"

Wilson shook his head in wonder. "Those cables were supposed to be indestructible. And *he*—that stupid brute, broke 'em like they were *nothing!* It's— it's impossible!"

Martin continued staring into the distance long after the Hulk had disappeared. "Yeah, well, that's the beauty of being that stupid, Max. The Hulk's too dumb to know that most of the things he does are impossible."

Chapter 2

NEW YORK ON A WINTER NIGHT HAS a strange, almost eerie feel to it. If, as on this night, a still-falling snow continues to cover the streets, the high-intensity street lamps cast harsh, angular shadows on deserted sidewalks. The occasional taxicab or bus that glides over the white-packed asphalt hisses almost silently between the darkened buildings, the snow seeming to absorb the sound, the lights shimmering in the falling crystals.

From the air, some thirty stories above the street, the scene seems even stranger. The few people that hurry huddled through the storm look distant and unreal in their land of cold shadows to the dark blue- and red-clad figure clinging to the stone facade of the Sperry Rand Building on 51st Street. *Well, one nice thing about the cold,* he thought as he shivered in the harsh December wind, *it tends to keep the criminal element indoors at night.*

And that makes this little friendly neighborhood Spider-Man about as useful as Custer's medic at Little Big Horn!

The youth called Spider-Man shivered again in the darkness high above the city. *The costume may be flashy, but it sure ain't gonna make it as the latest thing in winter wear! I wonder if any of the other superheroes in town wear long johns under their costumes?*

He lifted his arm and fired a thin strand of almost indestructible chemical webbing at the building across the street. It stuck to the stone face and Spider-Man leaped into the air. As he swung, he fired another strand from the web shooter under his gloves at the neon-lit facade of Radio City Music Hall.

He landed lightly on the snow-covered theater marquee and trotted along it until it turned to run along Sixth Avenue. *Guess I won't worry about that till tomorrow. As for tonight, I still have the thrilling prospect of several hours of studying and general book cracking before I grab me seventy or eighty winks.*

The Web-slinger swung smoothly up the quiet, deserted street. *At least the exercise's warming me up. Still, I wish I had pockets in this getup. A taxi'd be just as warm and a whole heck of a lot easier. But I doubt I could find a cabbie in this city who'd want to take an IOU from a guy wearing a mask!*

Spider-Man paused at 73rd Street, clinging by his fingers and toes to the face of a building as he caught his breath. He took in large lungfuls of cold, crisp air. *Hey! The pollution doesn't taste all that bad frozen!*

Suddenly, the Wall-crawler's masked face jerked up. His head began to tingle fiercely with the unmistakable sensation of his unique spider-sense, a sixth sense that warned Spider-Man whenever danger was present or nearby. In this instance, however, it was the latter, for, even as the tingling flared up in his skull, Spidey's eye caught a flash of light moving across the roof of the office building across Sixth Avenue.

Hello! Looks like studying's just been bumped from this eve's agenda, 'cause whatever light through yonder window breaks, it sure isn't the sun, and the way things work out in this business, I just ain't lucky enough for it to be my Juliet!

He swung across the street and scampered easily up the side of the building like the arachnid from which he took his name. Most lights inside were off. This late, even the most diligent of workers would be long gone.

Spider-Man peered carefully over the ledge to the roof. No one was there, but the fresh cover of snow was disturbed by many sets of footprints and the door to the stairs was ajar. *Looks like there're some late-night visitors on the prowl. Gee, I guess I've got my work cut out for me after all.*

It's so nice to feel wanted!

The Wall-crawler turned and started down the side of the building. He crisscrossed the facade, this time checking carefully in each office for sight of the burglars.

His search was quickly rewarded.

Spidey clung outside the eighteenth-floor window, watching as four black-clad intruders moved about inside with the aid of a pencil-thin light from a flashlight.

I don't know what's in there, but whatever it is, it's obviously worth stealing! So, no sense me hanging out here in the cold like a side of beef. . . .

Spider-Man swung onto the ledge outside the window and crouched there for several seconds. The intruders had stopped across the room before a heavy door marked "Private," their backs to the window. The man holding the flashlight knelt. He inserted a slim piece of wire into the lock and probed delicately. It was a considerably more complex lock than most people used on their front doors, so the task required all the tall man's attention. The others watched their leader tensely. They had not noticed the costumed figure perched outside, watching their every move through the opaque one-way lenses in his macabre mask.

But that would change soon enough.

The tall man felt the pick push against the tumblers until they were all properly aligned. Then, with a deft flick of the wrist, the lock clicked softly. A gentle nudge from the dark-garbed man and the door swung open. The kneeling man grinned to his companions.

"Piece o' cake," he whispered.

The man with the flashlight stood as the others filed by him into the office. Each man was dressed the same, in black slacks, turtle neck, and windbreaker. When the last man was in, the tall man, with a last look around the deserted office, followed them. The door snapped shut behind him.

A short, dark man with a black mustache said, "Okay, Jocko."

The tall man clapped his companion lightly on the shoulder. "It's going real smooth, Mandez," Jocko said, winking.

Mandez looked at his watch and frowned. "Yeah, well, we've got seven minutes to get the stuff and get back to the roof to meet the chopper."

"Relax, man," the big man smiled. "Ain't a safe been made that I can't crack in less'n half that time."

Jocko ran his hand along the wall by the door and found the light switch. When the lights came on, they saw they were in a large, windowless office, decorated in modern plastic and chrome. The desk was a clear-plastic top set on four curved shiny legs. Filing cabinets were gleaming steel; bookcases, crammed with well-read manuals and bulky computer readouts, were made of chrome tubes and Lucite shelves and assembled against a wall between framed reproductions of modern computer art.

"Okay, boys," Jocko grinned, rubbing his hands vigorously together. "Let's see where these turkeys hide their goodies."

The quartet spread out and began ransacking the

office, pulling drawers from cabinets, papers and books from shelves and pictures from walls. Within moments, the once-neat example of industrial interior decorating was reduced to a room full of smashed and twisted junk. A small safe stood exposed on the wall, the silver-framed picture that had covered it lying broken across the room.

Jocko stood before the safe. He had instantly recognized the make and model. Cracking it would be a cinch.

The tall man rubbed his fingertips lightly against his jacket. "All right, guys. Grab a bunch of papers from the cabinet there while I open this here cigar box. The man said to make 'em guess what we was after."

He began working on the safe, his trained fingers slowly twirling the dial as he kept his ear close to the thick metal door. Jocko had broken into a lot of safes in his day, but never, before this time, for anybody else. Now, tonight, he was using his valuable skills for a stranger, a man Jocko had never met. Orders came over the telephone. Money was left in unmarked envelopes in his mailbox. All very mysterious.

But whoever the guy was, his cash was green and that was what counted.

"Five minutes," Mandez whispered tensely, checking his watch for the fifth time in half a minute.

"You worry too much, Mandez," Jocko chuckled softly, concentrating on the delicate task at hand. He felt rather than heard the second tumbler click into place. "Now relax, man. I'll be inside this sorry excuse for a cracker box in a second."

Mandez nodded, consulting his watch again. Jocko was right. He was too jumpy tonight, though he didn't know why. Maybe it was the weird guy who hired them having insisted on so much secrecy and having the gang follow *his* timetable. The small dark man did not like it when he and his companions weren't in on the planning and didn't control the proceedings. He liked to handle things his way, otherwise he had the paranoid feeling that something just had to go wrong.

There was a knock at the door.

The four men froze. Mandez tiptoed over to the door and put his ear to it for several seconds, listening carefully as his hand snaked out and clicked off the overhead light.

"Well?" Jocko hissed impatiently in the sudden darkness, his fingers unmoving on the dial.

Mandez shrugged, his eyes shiny in the darkness. "I don't hear anything," he whispered back.

"Awright." Jocko clicked on the penlight and shone it on the safe. "Keep the lights off while I finish this." He snapped his fingers at the two men standing silently in the center of the room. "And you guys. Stand by the door—and don't use your guns unless you have to!"

The men started toward the door through the dark as Jocko turned his attention back to the safe. One more turn of the dial . . .

Click!

There was another knock, this one much louder.

"Jocko!"

The tall man turned to his companion. "Be cool, Mandez," he grinned, reaching under his dark windbreaker. He withdrew a pistol. "And don't keep our mystery guest waiting."

Mandez swallowed hard and yanked open the door.

"Say hey, Web-slinger fans! Spidey's here!" The Wall-crawler stood casually against the door frame, his arms folded across his chest. "I saw you kids still had your light on and wanted to know if I could join your pajama party."

"Spider-Man!" Mandez screeched.

Jocko cursed to himself. Those idiots hadn't given him any room in their carefully planned schedule to deal with trouble, especially trouble of this size. Keeping his eyes on Spider-Man, Jocko surreptitiously slid his hand into the safe and felt carefully around. His fingers closed around a small plastic case: a tape cassette. He quickly shoved it into his back pocket.

And now for Spider-Man.

The tall man moved away from the safe and aimed his gun at the Wall-crawler. "Maintain the pose, Spider-Man," he said slowly. "Me and my boys got what we came for and now we're leaving. Peacefully, *if* you let us, but don't think that means I've got anything against blowing your head off."

Spidey chuckled and stepped into the room. "My goodness gracious me, we *are* feeling hostile tonight, aren't we, Sluggo?"

"Go ahead and laugh, man," Jocko growled. "We'll see how much you laugh with the wind whistling through your face!"

Spider-Man put up his hands in a pacifying gesture. "You don't mean you plan to shoot me with *that* gun, do you?"

Jocko raised his gun higher. "Move out of the way, Spider-Man," he warned. "There ain't nothing wrong with this gun."

"Sure there is, friend," Spidey said. "There's all kinds of gunk clogging up the barrel." The Web-slinger curled the middle fingers of both hands to depress the two small buttons secreted beneath his gloves. Twin strands of webbing shot from the nozzles at his wrists and flew accurately across the room to their target.

Jocko pulled the trigger a split second later. The bullet struck the already-hardening webbing material and exploded, shattering the gun in the man's hand. He howled in pain and dropped the smoldering, ruined pistol.

"Gee, that was fun," Spider-Man said. "Anybody else wanna play with me for a while?"

"Damnit," Jocko screamed, cradling his wounded hand to his chest. "Get him, you idiots!"

" 'Get him'?" Spidey asked. " 'Get him'? Can't you creeps ever use some new material, y'know, something with a little snap and some of the old pizzazz.

You can't imagine how dull it gets listening to a whole bunch of clowns who sound like they learned to talk from a 1938 John Garfield movie."

The two black-clad men moved toward Spider-Man from the center of the room. The costumed youth's pose was casual but he was inwardly tensed, ready to move at the slightest provocation. And that came soon enough as the thug on Spidey's right lunged forward, his hands reaching for the Wall-crawler's throat. Spidey caught his wrists in his gloved hands.

"Hi, sailor," he said. "New in town?"

He moved at the exact second as the second thug, swinging the first man's body around to intercept a clenched fist. The captured man grunted in pain as the blow skipped off his ribs and he tried to pull free of Spidey's grasp.

Still holding tight, the Wall-crawler swept his booted foot past his captive and kicked the second thug in the shin. While the punk hopped on one foot holding his wounded leg, Spider-Man released the first man's wrists. The man looked in surprise into the staring white orbs for a moment and then smiled, drawing back his fist.

"Don't get cocky, punk," Spidey said.

His webbing shot out, snagging the man's raised hand. Spider-Man jerked the web leash forward, sending the startled burglar stumbling toward him. "Come to papa," the Web-slinger said lightly. The man's face smacked into Spidey's gloved hand with a sharp crack that sent his head snapping back. With a deep sigh, the thug crumpled to the floor.

Spider-Man turned to the other man who stood in the center of the room with a look of pain on his face and a gun in his hand. "Just what *is* this strange fascination you creeps have with those things?"

"They shut up wise guys, wise guy!" the man growled. He pulled the trigger.

The Wall-crawler was moving the instant he saw the thief tense to fire. He crouched and sprang up at the ceiling. His fingers touched the soundproofing material and stuck. He swung his legs up and plastered his body against the ceiling as the bullet whizzed harmlessly by beneath him. The crook cursed and re-adjusted his aim. Hanging by his feet, Spider-Man reached down and grabbed the gunman's arm. He pulled him off the floor.

"You really oughta see the view from up here, chuckles. It's simply breathtaking!"

The crook's feet kicked helplessly in the air, but the Wall-crawler's hold was firm—almost supernaturally strong. The man opened his mouth to speak, but the costumed youth stifled his words with a gag of web-bing. "No, don't speak," Spidey pleaded. "It'll just spoil the atmosphere."

More of the thick, viscous webbing was wrapped around his body until the burglar was thoroughly bound and Spider-Man could stick the still-struggling man to the ceiling like a giant caterpillar nestled in its cocoon.

The Web-slinger dropped to the floor and regarded the trussed-up thief. "Whew! Whenever you get out of that glop, junior," he said, shaking his head in dis-belief, "you're gonna be the biggest, ugliest butterfly anybody's ever seen!"

A sudden, sharp tingling in his head made Spider-Man whirl around, alert. It didn't take long for him to see what his spider-sense was trying to tell him: ex-cept for the two thugs he'd just fought, the vandalized office was empty.

Awww . . . heck!

Spidey ran toward the open door. *I was having so much fun with those goons I forgot about the other two. What would all my loyal fans say if they heard I let the bad guys get away, with the loot, yet!*

. . . Whatever the loot happens to be.

He raced out into the darkened outer office. To his right he heard the echo of rubber soles slapping rhyth-mically against a linoleum floor. Harsh, barely audible whispers followed the footsteps from the darkness.

"Jocko . . . ?"

"Yeah man, it's cool! I got it, I got it!"

Not for long if I've got any say in the matter, sweetums!

Spidey took off after the whispers. His uncanny spider-sense helped him avoid obstacles in the dark office as he followed silently behind the noisily retreating crooks. They were headed for the stairway to the roof.

The Web-slinger raised his hand, intending to ensnare the fleeing thieves in a sticky web. *Whoa, there, m'boy. Not so fast! I may as well make a couple of bucks out of this burglary even if the burglars won't! I'll let 'em get to the roof where I can get a couple of good shots of yours truly capturing the alleged perpetrators. I can always sell whatever I get to Jolly Jonah Jameson for the* Daily Bugle.

And even if he doesn't want to print them, they still make dandy dart boards.

Spidey chuckled to himself as he ran. *No wonder you were able to get to where you are today, Mr. Parker! You use the old noggin!*

Though the costumed youth could have easily caught up with, and, with little more effort, overtaken the thieves as they pounded up the narrow stairwell, he held back. He unclipped a miniature camera from his belt buckle and checked it over. *Okay, film's all loaded, shutter's on the right setting for night. . . . Okay gang, let's get ready to roll 'em! Action!*

The Web-slinger paused at the doorway and took a moment to web the small camera to the top of the frame. He pressed the automatic timer and heard the mechanism whirring, beginning to click off pictures of the burglars running across the roof.

They stopped by the edge of the roof, peering anxiously through the falling snow into the dark sky. "What's the time, Mandez?" Jocko demanded. "Where's the damn chopper?"

Mandez checked his wrist. "It'll be about another minute."

"Nope, guess again, clowns."

Spider-Man sauntered across the roof, smiling to himself beneath his mask.

"Huh?" Mandez whirled, pulling a pistol from his jacket pocket.

"I said you're wrong, bunky. You haven't got a minute," Spidey called to the trembling man as he walked evenly into the gun's range. "Matter of fact, your time is just about up."

"Jocko?"

"Kill 'im!" the tall man roared angrily. He tenderly clutched his throbbing hand to his stomach, gritting his teeth from the pain. The burglar was certain the exploding gun had broken several bones in addition to severely burning him.

"Do it, man! Shoot Spider-Man!"

Mandez reacted automatically and instantly to the shouted command by squeezing the trigger. His sights were set squarely on the eerie black spider emblem on the costumed crime-fighter's chest. At this range, the dark little man couldn't miss.

Spider-Man threw himself headlong across the mottled roof material, rolling his lithe body into a smoothly executed somersault until he stood on his hands before Mandez. His dark blue-clad legs pumped out and rammed into the short man's stomach. Mandez gasped, doubling over in pain. Spidey bounced to his feet and grabbed the thief by the front of his jacket before he could topple over.

"No matter what the National Rifle Association tells you about guns, cutie," he lectured patiently to the gasping, red-faced man, *"don't* believe them! You've just had a firsthand taste of how badly a person can get hurt because of them." He let the moaning thief slide to the ground.

Spider-Man faced Jocko and folded his arms across his chest. "Well, looks like it's just you and me now, babe. You wanna surrender peaceably or do I have to play patty-cake on your face with my fist first?"

Jocko opened his mouth to snarl a reply, but at that moment, both men noticed a hard roar that filled

the night sky, a sound that mere moments before had
been a distant noise in the background.

A light shone suddenly from the sky, like a search-
light piercing a white-specked black curtain, and a
helicopter, its flying lights flashing red and white
against the roof, descended toward them. Spider-Man
stepped back, gasping in surprise.

*You should've guessed it, Web-head! How else
would these turkeys get on and off the top of a
twenty-two-story building in a hurry? Only problem
now is where the heck do I get a flyswatter big
enough to take care of that thing?*

The copter hovered a dozen feet above the roof,
its whirling blades whipping up a cloud of powdery
snow. Then it began to descend as a rope ladder was
lowered from the cabin.

The Web-slinger was blinded by the whirlpool of
snow and all but swept off his feet by the force of the
powerful downdraft stirred up by the unmarked aircraft's thumping propellers. But he managed to stay
upright and fight against the wind toward the spot
where Jocko had last stood.

His hands closed on empty air.

Awwww—

The costumed youth heard the hovering chopper's
engine change pitch above him. Slowly, the brutal
smash of air on Spidey's back let up, finally disappearing, as the aircraft rose smoothly from the roof.
He caught sight of Jocko's black-clad legs being hauled
into the cabin before the copter veered off and receded
swiftly into the night.

—shoot!

Spider-Man stared into the snow-filled night long
after the helicopter was gone from sight. He sighed,
his breath steaming out in a wisp of smoke. He
turned, brushing the dusty powder from his costume,
and walked back across the roof to the door and his
still-clicking camera. He pulled it free from its hiding
place above the door and weighed it absently in his
hand.

I suppose the cops would appreciate knowing about this little midnight get together—though if I had my druthers, I'd druther nobody found out how I screwed it up. Bad press is the last thing in the world I need!

He sighed again and tucked the tiny camera into his belt and started down the stairs.

Besides, if I kept these action-packed photos to myself, I wouldn't get paid!

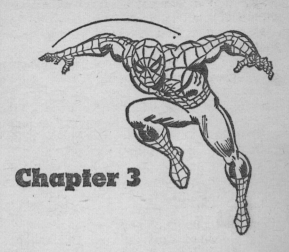

Chapter 3

FIFTEEN MINUTES LATER, SPIDER-MAN swung lightly onto another snow-covered roof over Manhattan. He landed behind the billboard-sized logo of the *Daily Bugle* that hung like a beacon in a sea of snow. He hurried, shivering all the way, to the unlocked door to the stairs.

Woof! I didn't think it was possible, but it's getting colder. New York will probably be knee-deep in snow tomorrow, which means things like taxis and buses won't be able to get around, which means the city will probably come to a standstill . . . unless they've got Spidey power to help get them from here to there!

Spidey stepped into the stairwell and quietly closed the door. A single bulb lit the small landing. He leaped up to the ceiling and clung there while he pried the cover off a nearby ventilator shaft.

Here's hoping the Bugle *doesn't employ any over-anxious cleaning ladies who do the vent shafts to . . . ahh!*

He pulled a package wrapped in old newspaper and string from the dusty shaft, replaced the cover and dropped to the floor. Then he reached up and pulled off his mask.

Peter Parker ran his hand through his tangled brown hair before tearing open the package. Inside was a set of clothing which Peter began slipping over his costume. *Bless you, wash 'n wear!* He removed his gloves and folded them neatly into his back pocket. *Since I started leaving a set of clothes here at the* Bugle *I've had a lot fewer hassles getting around, even if a lot of folks here are beginning to think I only own one shirt!*

When he finished dressing, Peter trotted down the stairs to the top floor, deserted now, far past midnight, and switched to the elevator to the forty-second floor. *With any luck whatsoever, the Idi Amin of the New York publishing set won't be here this late.*

Peter stepped from the elevator into the subdued atmosphere of the *Bugle*'s city room. Most of the desks were deserted, their typewriters covered for the night. The cleaning crew had already been through the room, emptying wastebaskets that, during the day, overflowed with crumpled wads of *Bugle* copy paper and crushed Styrofoam coffee cups. A lone copyboy weaved through the deserted desks with an armload of the day's first edition, tossing the freshly printed copies on the few occupied desks. The reporters manning those desks put aside their work and leaned back with their feet up to read leisurely the fruits of their day's labors.

The great information-gathering beast was, for the moment, at rest.

Peter waved to the one or two familiar faces on the night shift as he walked through the long, brightly lit room. He could see the lights were also on in Joe Robertson's office. Peter rapped on the door and opened it several inches.

"Anybody home?" he asked, looking inside.

The middle-aged black man seated behind the desk

in the generous-sized office looked up from the papers
in his hand. "Peter," he said in surprise. "What brings
you here in the dead of night?"

"I can't help it, Robbie," Peter grinned, stepping inside. "I got homesick for the company of the talented
and lovely J. Jonah Jameson, so I thought I'd bop on
by and say howdy."

"Why do I doubt that?" the *Daily Bugle*'s city editor
laughed. He leaned back comfortably in his chair and
picked up his pipe from the desk. "However, if you'd
really like to see our fearless leader . . ."

"No, no thanks, Robbie," Peter said quickly. "It's
too soon since I last ate to risk it."

Robbie filled his pipe from a leather pouch. "Then
what, may I ask without sounding ungracious, *does*
bring you here, Pete?"

Peter fished in his shirt pocket and came up with a
small roll of film. "Ah, yes, my friend," he said in his
best, none-too-good, W.C. Fields impersonation. "It is
late, but the evil perpetrators of vicious deeds of ne'er-
do-well work not by the clock. Witness this, the evi-
dence."

"That was *awful!*" Robbie chuckled, lighting his
pipe.

"The *shtick* or the photos?"

"Let me put it this way, son," Robbie said, thoughtfully puffing on his pipe. "You don't see us paying you
for your comedy routines, do you? And speaking of
that which we *do* pay you for, what have you got?"

Peter winked at the city editor. "Touché," he
laughed. "But seriously, folks. There was a . . ."

"*Robertson!*"

The door flew open and crashed into the wall as J.
Jonah Jameson stormed angrily into the room, a piece
of teletype copy clutched in his tightly clenched fist.
"Robertson," the grizzled, gray-haired publisher of the
Daily Bugle fumed. "Do you know what this is?"

Robertson's dark features remained passive despite
his boss's tirade. J. Jonah Jameson was not the easiest
man in the world to work for, but when it came down

to publishing a first-rate newspaper, there was no better man. His temper was, as far as Robbie was concerned, just another part of the job.

"Looks like something off the wire, Jonah. Is it important?"

Jameson planted himself in front of the city editor's desk and fixed Robbie with a look that would have withered a lesser man. "Oh, no, not really," he growled sarcastically. "It's just that there was a break-in at a government-employed computer-processing firm not a mile and a half from here and the wires got to it before we did!"

"Then I'd better get on the stick," Joe Robertson replied, reaching for the telephone.

"No need to waste your dime, Robbie," Peter piped in. "I've already got the story for you."

Jameson flinched at the sound of Peter's voice and turned slowly. He took in the young photographer seated behind him and groaned. "Parker, for crying out loud! Don't you ever go home and sleep?" He turned to Robbie. "What? Has he got a cot in the back room or something? Why the hell is he always around whenever . . ."

"Nice to see you too, Mr. J.," Peter cut in dryly.

"What *is* it with this kid?" Jameson pleaded with Robbie. "How come he's always around here, like a bill collector? I can't even get away from him in the middle of the night."

"Uh, Jonah."

"What?"

Robbie calmly struck a match and relit his cold pipe. "I believe the boy has something for us on that very subject."

"Does he really?" Jameson scowled at Peter. "Why don't you let the rest of us in on it then?"

Peter settled comfortably in the chair and smiled. "Well, since you asked so nice. You see, there I was, walking along the street, just minding my own business, mind you, when . . ."

"Get *on* with it, Parker!"

"Remember your blood pressure, Mr. J.," Peter warned. "Anyway," he hurried on before the dour-faced publisher could reply, "I caught sight of a fracas on a roof on 72nd and rushed up there for pictures. And what did I find but your friend and mine, Spider-Man . . ."

"That *name* again!" Jameson groaned, slapping a hand over his eyes.

"I knew you'd be pleased. So, Spidey did a little breaking and entering on their heads but, just like the movies, a helicopter made a daring rescue and I'll bet you'll never guess who got pictures of the whole she-bang."

"Think you're real clever, don't you, kid?" Jameson asked snidely.

Peter shrugged. "Moderately so, compared to the next guy. Especially when you consider the guys I'm usually next to."

"Then how come, smarty, you didn't stick around long enough to get a few of the facts? Like the fact that the company robbed was engaged in work for the government, specifically NASA. Like the fact that it appears the burglars were after the newly completed programming material for NASA's next unmanned space shot. Like the fact that they somehow got away with the loot even though the cops got three of them." Jameson fished a cigar from his vest pocket and jammed it in his mouth as he glared at Peter.

The young photographer grinned sheepishly. "Oh, didn't I mention? It seems, ah, that one of them got away from Spider-Man."

Jameson's hand, holding a lighted match halfway to his cigar, halted in midair. "Did you say Spider-Man let one of them get away?"

"He didn't *let* the guy get away, he just managed to . . ."

"Forget it. Did you get pictures of Spider-Man blowing it?" He gasped as the match burned down to his fingers and dropped it to the carpet.

"Uh, yeah, but there are also some of . . ."

A smile spread sickeningly across Jameson's face as he finally touched another match to the top of his cigar. "Did you hear that, Robbie?" he puffed contentedly.

Robbie smiled thinly. "I heard, Jonah."

His boss's fanatical hatred of the Web-slinger was legendary in New York. A week did not go by without the *Bugle* at least once sporting headlines in large type about the menace the costumed crime-fighter posed to the city. Robbie had watched as, over the years, that hatred had grown, until it was almost all-consuming. But, like Jameson's temper tantrums, it had become so much a part of everyday routine that the city editor hardly noticed it anymore.

Jameson grinned broadly, puffing happily on an El Ropo special. Peter thought the older man's face would crack under the unaccustomed strain of previously unexercised muscles being brought into play. *Seeing Jameson smile is about as rare as a tap-dancing mud shark—though not nearly as pretty!* "I might be interested in buying those pictures, kid," Jameson said.

"I had a hunch you might, Mr. Jameson." Peter held up the roll of film.

Jameson plucked the film from Peter's hand. He chuckled. "You'll be happy to hear that your photographs are going to be on page one of the next edition, Parker. A little recognition oughta make a snotty punk like you real happy."

"In lieu of more money, it'll do, I guess," Peter Parker said.

"Good." Jameson started for the door, whistling tunelessly to himself.

"You're really enjoying this, aren't you," Peter said.

"Enormously, Parker. I love it when that damned Wall-crawler falls flat on his foolish red-masked face." The grizzled publisher allowed himself a short laugh at his nemesis' misfortune and left.

"Get him," Peter scoffed. "I'll bet he's a real laugh riot at funerals and natural disasters."

Joe Robertson tapped a pencil against his desk.

"Oh, don't let Jonah bug you, Pete," he smiled. "Beneath that rough, gruff exterior . . ."

". . . is a rough, gruff man." Peter stood and jammed his hands in his pockets. "Believe me, Robbie. I've learned to live quite well with the fact that Jolly Jonah would rather see the Internal Revenue man come around to do an audit than me." He grinned. "Heck, considering the people he *likes,* I like to think of his hating me as sort of a status symbol."

Robbie stood and came around to the front of the desk. "Glad to see you're taking it so well. Come on, I'll buy you a cup of coffee. It tastes awful, but it's cheap."

"No thanks," Peter smiled. "I've had the coffee here before and my doctor warned me never to let it happen again. Naw, I think I'll just mosey on home and grab some sleep. It's already way past my bedtime."

"Mine too, actually."

"Yeah, what are you and Jameson doing here this late anyway?"

"The regular night man's out sick tonight so I drew double duty. As for Jonah," Joe Robertson inclined his head toward the *Bugle* publisher and editor-in-chief, bent over a teletype machine in a glass-enclosed office, reading the latest bulletin clattering over the wires. "It's hard to say about him. He's about as dedicated a newsman as I've ever met and I guess this newspaper's about the most important thing in his life. He spends a lot of nights here."

Peter could sense the dedication Robbie felt toward his boss. No matter what hassles Jameson put him through, his city editor remained loyal. True, there were less headaches and more money waiting for him at any number of papers across the country, but, like J. Jonah Jameson, Robbie was a dedicated newsman. And most of the action happened at the *Daily Bugle.*

Jameson tore a strip of yellow paper from the wire and rushed across the room. He spotted Robbie and hurried over, brandishing the paper.

Without a word, he handed the copy to Robbie.

Joe Robertson scanned the typewritten report and his forehead creased into a deep frown as he read. "Interesting," he muttered, chewing on the stem of his pipe.

"What's up?" Peter wanted to know.

"Seems somebody broke into an office at the Johnson Space Center in Houston, Texas about an hour ago," Robbie said, looking up. "The only thing they took, according to this report, was some new data having to do with an upcoming unmanned flight."

"Sound familiar, Parker?" Jameson asked, blowing a stream of blue, pungent smoke toward the young photographer.

Peter coughed, nodding in agreement as he turned red. *I'll be . . . two robberies involving NASA materials on the same planned flight taking place on the same night. Maybe coincidence does stretch pretty far at times. . . .*

But if it does, how come my spider-sense is tingling like the Kingpin was breathing down my neck?

Chapter 4

HE FELT COLD.

He could not understand how that was so.

His last thoughts, seen through an emerald haze in his muddled consciousness, were of great heat. A sea of shimmering gold stretched endlessly before him.

And rage.

But now the heat was gone, the yellow sea receded.

And the rage spent.

He wrapped his thin arms around his narrow chest, shivering in the bitter cold. He could feel the hard, frozen ground against his back, the chill of metal against his neck. With a moan, he drew his knees up to his chest. But the biting cold would not go away.

And then he awoke.

It took Dr. Robert Bruce Banner several seconds to pry his tired, bloodshot eyes open. The lids felt like lead, his whole body heavy with fatigue as if some sort of parasite had drained the last iota of strength from his frail body.

41

And in a way, of course, that was exactly what had happened.

The cold winter sun sent a stab of pain through the handsome young scientist's dark eyes. He groaned miserably. But it was always this way, he thought. Always the same painful weakness, the same fear and uncertainty.

Where had he been?

What havoc had he wreaked this time?

And where, in God's name, was he now?

Bruce Banner rose slowly, leaning against the brick wall for support. He saw he was in an alleyway. He had been asleep against the wall, curled in the fetal position with his neck pressed against one of the many trash cans that shielded him from view from the street. As usual after one of these episodes, the young scientist was clothed in nothing but the tattered remains of his trousers, worn and stretched out of shape about his waist.

He staggered from the alley onto what was obviously the main street of a small town. The two-lane thoroughfare was clean, the stores that lined it neat and homey looking. Across the street from where he stood, Bruce could see a drugstore, an insurance agent and real-estate office, a dress shop, a small movie theater, and an ice-cream parlor. He was somewhere in the midwest, he decided.

Bruce leaned against the cold wall, shivering. He had to get some clothes, get into something warm before he froze to death. He didn't know the exact date, he seldom did anymore, but he was sure it was sometime in late December, probably just after Christmas. Time had little meaning to Bruce Banner these days. It merely represented an extension of torment to the young scientist; that many more times it would happen, his curse. That many more times that anger or frustration would build in him, causing the change to take place in his body until he was no longer Bruce Banner.

Until he became the awesome Hulk!

Bruce shuddered in a chill wind. Forget all that

now, he told himself. It's over—if only for the time being. For now, I've got to get organized and get my hands on some clothing!

He shoved his hands into his ragged pockets and felt around for the small wad of paper he knew was pinned there. He pulled it free and brought the five twenty-dollar bills out. It was money he tried to keep on him at all times for just such situations. He never knew where he would wind up after a spell as the Hulk, but he was always sure he would need the money.

The street was empty. From the position of the sun in the sky, Bruce could tell it was just after eight in the morning, at least an hour before the townspeople would be up and about in the streets of the small town. He rubbed his goosefleshed skin as he hurried up the street. As he suspected, there was a men's clothing store between the post office and green grocer. Hand-printed signs in the window advertised professional tailoring, dry cleaning, and several brands of blue jeans. It also noted that Fletcher's Men's Wear opened its doors to the public at nine each morning. A big red "Closed" sign hung in the window. Bruce could not wait an hour.

He began pounding on the glass door, hoping the proprietor was either in early or lived in the rear of the shop.

"Hello," he shouted. "Anybody here?"

"Coming, coming," a man called from inside. "Don't break down the door."

Bruce huddled in the doorway, slapping his thin arms for warmth. Hurry, damn you, he thought angrily.

The shade was lifted from over the glass and a round, red face peered out at him. The little man started at first sight of the ragged young man. "What'd you want, mister? I don't open for about an hour yet."

"I need to buy some clothes," Bruce called through chattering teeth. "It . . . it's an emergency."

The face looked him up and down. "Look, I'm sorry, but . . ."

Bruce pulled the hundred dollars from his pocket and waved it in front of the man's face. "I've got the money to pay," he cried.

The little man, obviously Mr. Fletcher, pursed his lips and looked the half-naked young man over one more time. At last he nodded, disappearing behind the shade. In seconds, the lock clicked and the door swung open.

"You're sure a mess, mister," Fletcher said, shaking his balding head. "What happened to you?"

Bruce stepped quickly inside, the warmth of the small, dark shop enveloping him like a thick, comfortable blanket. He closed his eyes in relief.

"Mister?"

"Mmm? Oh, I'm sorry."

"I said," the man repeated in a slow, midwestern drawl, "that you look awful. Been in an accident?"

"Yes." Bruce nodded. "Yes, you could say that," he muttered softly.

Fletcher frowned. "Well, have you been to the police?"

"There's nothing the police could do." He laughed bitterly. "I don't think there's anything anybody can do."

Jim Fletcher stared hard at the young man. He had always felt he was a fairly shrewd judge of character, that he could size up a man in a glance. But this time . . . well, maybe he'd been a bit hasty letting this one in.

Banner sensed the little man's shift in reaction to his strange appearance and even stranger manner and smiled quickly to compensate. "Listen," he said lightly. "It really wasn't anything serious, though it didn't do my clothes any good as you can see." He laughed. "But nobody was hurt."

Fletcher nodded slowly. "Sure. What can I do for you?"

"The works, I guess. Nothing too expensive,

though." He held up the money. "I'm on a fairly tight budget."

Within minutes, Bruce Banner was stepping from a dressing room in the rear of the shop, dressed in a blue-denim work shirt, blue jeans, and warm, heavy hiking boots. Just being dressed again made him feel better, almost forgetting that mere hours ago he had been a rampaging engine of destruction, doing things he would only find out about if he chanced on a newspaper article or television newscast recounting his activity.

Bruce selected some extra underwear, socks, and a spare shirt, as well as a small overnight bag which, along with a warm, down parka, he bought. The purchases left him with less than twenty dollars in his pocket.

Mr. Fletcher directed Bruce to the drugstore up the street when the young scientist asked him about a place to eat. Thanking the little man, Bruce left the clothing shop. He was warm now, and his mind and body both felt better for it. The horror of his other self did not seem as nightmarish with the simple addition of warm clothing. Maybe, he thought, the clothes *do* make the man.

Or maybe they merely served to hide the truth and make the facade more presentable.

A small bell tinkled over the door as Bruce stepped into the drugstore. The word that sprang immediately to the young scientist's mind as he looked the store over was "quaint." Against the far wall stood an old, well-used display counter behind which worked the white-coated pharmacist. A long display rack with magazines, newspapers, and comic books shared another wall with a cosmetics display. Opposite that was a lunch counter with six of the eight stools filled by men eating breakfast. Through the center of the store ran racks filled with toiletries and household items. Old signs still hung on the walls, signs advertising products Bruce remembered from his childhood but that had long since vanished or changed over the years, and signs for soft drinks and patent medicines that would have been familiar to his parents.

The young scientist smiled genuinely for the first time that day. He recalled a drugstore much like this one from his childhood, in the small town his grandparents lived in. Memories of hot summer afternoons spent reading crisp, new comic books while sipping a huge ice-cream soda in the cool of the dark little store flooded his mind. That was a simpler time—a better time.

Bruce scooped up a copy of the only newspaper in the rack and went over to the counter. He hung his new parka on one of the hooks against the wall and took a seat next to a small, nervous-looking man wearing a gray suit several sizes too large for his bony frame. He was the only man seated there not clad in overalls and muddy, battered work shoes. He glanced up quickly when Bruce sat down next to him. He snubbed out the nonfiltered cigarette he was smoking and concentrated on his cup of coffee.

"Good morning," Bruce smiled pleasantly.

The man stopped his coffee cup halfway to his mouth and snapped his head in Banner's direction. "Oh?"

"Relatively so, at least," Bruce conceded, extending his hand. "Name's Banner. Bruce Banner."

The nervous little man slowly replaced his cup and took the proffered hand for a brief, limp shake. "Oh. Ernest Hughes." He took a loud sip of coffee. "I own the insurance place down the street."

"I'm just passing through myself." Bruce glanced down at the masthead of the newspaper on the counter. *The MacDermont Chronicle-Eagle,* he read. MacDermont Point, Kansas.

Kansas?

Last he remembered, he had been in Nevada.

The Hulk really gets me around, he thought bitterly.

"Oh?" Hughes reached for another cigarette from the pack in his jacket pocket and lighted it.

"Yes," Bruce said. "Although I *have* been thinking

of finding a place to settle down for a while. And this town, well . . . it seems to fit the bill pretty nicely." Now what made me say that? Bruce thought. He'd never had any such thoughts, but even as he heard himself say it, he realized it might be what he was looking for after all. How long had he roamed the country seeking a cure from science for his curse? Maybe it was time he sought a cure in himself. In a town like MacDermont Point, Kansas, there could be little to cause the dreaded anxiety that triggered his metamorphosis.

"Oh. Yes, Mr. Banner. We've quite a friendly community in MacDermont Point," he said, his voice full of either civic pride or professional interest in the young man as a potential customer for his real-estate office. "Very neighborly, very peaceful."

"Peaceful." Bruce Banner savored the word. "That's what I'm looking for."

The waitress came hurrying over from the kitchen through a door behind the counter with a plate full of fried eggs, sausages, and home-fried potatoes. Bruce Banner watched with hungry eyes as she passed him and placed it before a burly man in overalls. He hadn't realized how hungry he was until he saw the food.

The waitress wiped her hands on the seat of her yellow uniform and looked up the counter. She saw Bruce and smiled. She was a pretty girl in her early twenties, tall and slim and quite beautiful. Her long, striking red hair was tied back in a ponytail. Her pretty green eyes sparkled.

"Hi," she said, full of cheer. "How're you today?"

"Fine," he smiled back. "And you?"

"Great. Can I get you something?"

He laughed. "Food."

She laughed with him, a bright, sweet sound. "Should I bring out one portion or should I keep it comin' until you tell me to stop?"

"That's not a bad idea," the young scientist grinned.

"But first, let's see how I do with a couple of scrambled eggs, bacon, and heaps of home fries and toast."

She nodded and went to the kitchen to place his order and then came back to fill his coffee cup. "You from around here, mister?" she asked.

He shook his head and gingerly tasted the hot, black liquid. Bruce couldn't remember anything ever tasting so good. "No," he said at last. "I suppose you could say I'm on the road."

"Really?" She brightened. "I love to travel," she said, leaning on the counter. "Not that I get to do all that much of it, mind you. You been to a lot of places?"

"I get around," Bruce admitted. "Er, by the way, I'm Bruce."

"My name's Shannon. You staying in town, Bruce?"

"Maybe," he shrugged. "It all depends on whether or not I can find a job and a place to stay. Actually, it all depends on the job, otherwise a place to stay is out of my range."

A bell rang in the kitchen. "Be right back," Shannon said. She disappeared into the back room and was back in a moment with Bruce's breakfast. He dug in.

Shannon watched him eat with a bemused smile. "Looks like you don't get to eat all that often."

"It's been a while," he said between mouthfuls.

"I'll bet. Hey, what kind of work is it you do anyway?"

Bruce put the last of the potatoes into his mouth and washed it down with a swallow of coffee. "Just about anything, actually. Farm work, construction, handiwork, small repairs. I'm what you might call a jack-of-all-trades, master-of-none."

"Can the jack jerk?"

"Come again?"

"Do you think you can handle soda jerking?"

"Sure. I mean, I don't see why not," he shrugged. Mixing an ice-cream soda, he thought, had to be easier than mixing chemicals. "Why? Do you know of a job somewhere?"

"Yeah. Here."

"Here?"

"Sure. It doesn't pay much, but you get all the banana splits you can eat," she grinned. "What d'you say, Bruce?"

"What else can I say? You've got yourself a soda jerk, lady." They shook hands across the counter. "Shouldn't I talk to the boss about this?"

"Don't have to do that. He trusts me to do all the hiring."

"Oh yeah? You manage the store for him?"

"Kind of. The boss is my father."

"Ah," Bruce smiled. "The boss's daughter."

"That's right, buster," she snarled playfully. "So don't get any ideas about trying your city-slicker ways on me."

"Don't worry, ma'am. I'm just a country boy at heart.

"Hey, Shannon," Bruce said. "I really appreciate the job. That's half my troubles down."

Shannon smiled. "How'd you like me to make that two out of two?"

"An apartment?"

"Well, not exactly an apartment," she laughed. "More like a room, but it's in a good boardinghouse not far from here. And I know there's an available room that I'm sure you can get."

Bruce raised an eyebrow. "Really," he said. "I suppose it's run by your grandmother, right?"

"Don't be silly, Bruce," she said. "Mom owns the house."

Chapter 5

THE PLAIN RED-BRICK HOUSE ON WAR-
ren Street stood behind a white picket fence in a yard
shaded by two large, stately elm trees, bare now of
their leaves. Bruce swung open the gate and walked
to the front door after checking the address against the
one Shannon had scrawled on the back of a paper
napkin.

He rang the doorbell.

A grayer, heavier, and older version of Shannon answered after the first ring. "Yes?" she inquired pleasantly.

"Mrs. O'Neal?"

"Yes."

"My name's Bruce Banner, ma'am."

"Oh, yes," the woman stepped back from the door
and gestured for Bruce to enter. "Shannon called me
and told me about you, Mr. Banner."

Bruce followed Shannon's mother into the warm,

pleasant house. They passed through the parlor, a room full of overstuffed, antique-looking chairs and sofas and little bric-a-brac scattered on shelves and atop the grand piano that stood in front of the window. They went down a narrow hallway to the stairs with Mrs. O'Neal chattering away a mile a minute about the splendor of MacDermont Point the whole time. She asked the young stranger any number of questions but did not seem the least bit interested in waiting to hear his replies before rushing on with her commentary and gossip.

Bruce Banner liked her immediately.

"There are four boarders living here, Mr. Banner, along with Shannon, Mr. O'Neal, and myself," she said showing him the second-floor room.

Bruce nodded, looking around the room. It was large enough for one person, with a bed, a chest of drawers, a small writing desk, and a closet—with just enough space left to move around. The oriental rug on the floor was worn threadbare in some spots from too many years of feet, and the furniture was old, but well kept. In all, the room was comfortable and, like the rest of this Kansas town, very warm.

"Do you like it, Mr. Banner? The rent's twenty dollars a week and that includes breakfast and dinner. And I'm sure you'll like our other boarders. There's Mr. Abernathy, the retired dry-goods man; Miss Pritchard, the grammar-school teacher; Mr. Walsh, the young law clerk; and Mrs. Taylor, Andy's widow. A fine group pf people."

"It's wonderful, Mrs. O'Neal. I'm sure I'll be very comfortable here," Bruce jumped in when the woman paused for a breath.

"I'm so glad," the woman beamed. "Shannon said you were a nice young man."

Bruce's eyebrows went up. "Did she?"

"My, yes. She spoke very highly of you." She leaned in close to Bruce and whispered conspiratorially. "Frankly, I'm glad she's finally showing some interest in young men. Shannon's never seemed very interested in the boys in town."

Bruce smiled, well aware that he was in for this wonderful little woman's life story unless he did something fast. "Well, thank you, Mrs. O'Neal. Now, I think I'd like to take a little nap, if you don't mind."

"Of course, Mr. Banner. Shall we see you for dinner?"

"Does, eh, Shannon usually eat at home?" he asked casually.

"Oh, yes."

Bruce smiled. "Then I'm looking forward to it, ma'am."

After dinner, Bruce Banner sat comfortably back in an overstuffed chair in the warm parlor reading a newspaper from Topeka, supplied by Dan Walsh, the young lawyer and his fellow boarder. Dinner had been as pleasant as he had anticipated, seated across the table from the radiant Shannon, chatting amicably with his new friends in the town of MacDermont Point.

Now, Shannon and her mother were in the kitchen doing the dishes and Mr. O'Neal was locked away in his den with his drugstore's books. Bruce sat across from Walsh, in the parlor. Walsh was a pudgy young man with a crew cut and a loud bow tie. Across from him sat Miss Daisy Pritchard, a very tidy-looking woman in her mid-thirties who seemed determined to live out her life as the stereotypical schoolmarm. Mrs. Beatrice Taylor, the widow, was a white-faced old lady who wore her silver hair in a tight bun on the top of her head. She dozed next to the radio, dressed in mourning black even though, Mrs. O'Neal had whispered to Bruce in confidence, her husband had been dead for almost twenty years. Finally there was Hank Abernathy, a hardy old gentleman who talked to Bruce enthusiastically throughout dinner about his days in the dry-goods business.

But Bruce had not minded the banal chatter in the least. He was happy with his new job and home and, especially, Shannon O'Neal. After the years he had spent on the run, on his quest for freedom, he realized he missed the security and stability of a home and people he could share a life with. Perhaps here, he could find some of the happiness he craved.

Perhaps.

Shannon came into the room. "You seem to be fitting in nicely, Mr. Banner," she said, standing over his chair.

"Feel right at home," he said laying the newspaper in his lap. "And I haven't had a meal like the one your mother served up in I don't know how long."

"She can certainly set a table," Shannon said. "How would you like to walk off some of that food?"

"Sounds nice," Bruce said, happy for the opportunity to be alone with her.

"Great. Give me fifteen minutes to help mom finish cleaning up and then I'll treat you to the fifty-cent tour of the town."

Bruce watched Shannon O'Neal walk from the parlor with a small, private smile on his lips. He let his mind wander, trying to envision a life in MacDermont Point. It wasn't a difficult image to conjure. She seemed to be everything he might want in a woman, and beautiful as well. He found it easy to see in his mind's eye a white picket fence surrounding a wooden frame house—his own—on one of the town's tree-lined streets. Children played happily in the front yard, rushing to greet Bruce as he came up the walk at night. And Shannon—she came from the house and . . .

He shook his head suddenly, a sad frown creasing his forehead.

How could he think such things? A normal life was forever closed to him. As long as the threat of the fearsome creature within him existed, ready to rear its monstrous head at any instant, his life could never be normal.

With a somber sigh, he closed his mind to those thoughts and returned his concentration to the news-

paper. He skimmed through the local section, searching the pages for any items relating to his alter ego's
activities during his last blackout.

The paper mentioned nothing of the Hulk, but a
small story on page eighteen caught his attention. He
read the small headline twice, not believing his eyes:

RESEARCHERS ANNOUNCE BREAKTHROUGH IN GAMMA-RAY CURE

It was only a few lines, but they were lines that
made the young scientist hold his breath in nervous
anticipation.

> (Chicago) Scientists at the Institute for Ra-
> diation Research (IRR) based in Chicago
> announced today a remarkable new cure
> for victims of deadly gamma-ray radiation.
> The cure, according to IRR spokesman,
> Dr. Daniel Irvine, is "a major break-
> through in the fight against radiation sick-
> ness." In a paper released this morning, Dr.
> Irvine said that while they are certain of
> their research, additional volunteers are
> still being sought for new studies. Volun-
> teers should contact the IRR at their offices
> at 823 LaSalle Street in Chicago.

Bruce slowly folded the paper, his eyes staring
blankly into space. Was it possible? Could it be true?
he wondered. Could some unknown researcher in
Chicago have come up with the answer to the question that had plagued him these many years?

Could it be possible that his long nightmare was
nearing an end?

"I've got to get to Chicago," he muttered suddenly,
almost leaping from his seat. He hurried past the startled boarders in the parlor and started up the stairs.
He stopped, his foot hovering in midair. You can't

just leave like this, he told himself; *not* without telling anyone—without telling Shannon. He turned and went into the kitchen where Shannon and Mrs. O'Neal stood washing dishes.

"Excuse me," he said. "Mrs. O'Neal. Shannon."

The two women turned.

"You shouldn't be in here," the older woman said with mock sternness. "This is women's work."

Bruce stepped forward. "I'm sorry," he said, looking into Shannon's sparkling green eyes. "I . . . I have to leave."

"Leave?" Shannon laughed in surprise. "That's ridiculous, Bruce. You just got here."

"I know," he said miserably. "And I wish I could stay longer, *much* longer, but it's imperative I get to Chicago as soon as possible." He spread his hands in a helpless gesture. "I wish I could explain it to you, but I can't. Not now. But believe me, it's terribly important to me."

Shannon lowered her eyes to the floor. "Oh. I see."

"Shannon, I don't like this any more than . . ."

"Oh, this *is* a shame, Mr. Banner." Mrs. O'Neal shook her head. "We so enjoy having new people around the house. Don't we, Shannon?"

The young woman's eyes rose and locked on Bruce's. "Yes, Mom," she said softly. "We do."

"I hope you understand, Shannon," Bruce said.

"I know," she smiled. "You have to."

"Well." Bruce cleared his throat, not knowing what else he could say. "I'll say good-bye, then." He started to leave but stopped at the door. "I . . . I almost forgot, Mrs. O'Neal. What do I owe you for today?"

The plump woman waved her hand before her, dismissing the subject. "Phsst," she said. "Forget that, Mr. Banner. I can't rightly charge you anything without your even having spent the night."

Bruce smiled fondly. "Thank you, ma'am," he said. "You're a nice person. Good-bye." He looked at Shannon. "Good-bye."

" 'Bye."

56   MURDERMOON

Bruce pushed through the kitchen door and hurried up to his room. It only took a minute to toss his few possessions into the overnight bag and shrug into his heavy parka. The young scientist wanted to get out of this house fast, before it became too hard to go.

Shannon was standing by the front door when he came downstairs.

He stopped several feet before her. "Well . . ." This was not the time to say what he really wanted to, he knew. Too much uncertainty still existed in his tumultuous life for him to make any commitment to anyone. Perhaps if his journey to Illinois was successful. But not now.

"I wanted you to know I'm sorry you can't stay, Bruce," she said.

He nodded, jamming his hands into his coat pockets. "I wouldn't go if I didn't have to, Shannon. I like it here."

She looked at him hard. "Whatever's in Chicago must be awfully important then."

"It is. It's what I've been looking for for a good many years."

"I see." The young woman studied her slender hands for several seconds. She seemed to be having difficulty saying what was on her mind. Finally, she looked up. "Will you be coming back? Someday, I mean?"

Bruce shrugged. Lord, after only twelve hours in town, why did this hurt so much? "Maybe. Maybe if I'm lucky this time and find what I'm looking for. I don't know."

She stepped aside and put her hand on the door-knob. "Good luck, Bruce." Shannon opened the door. The night air blew cold across his face.

"Good-bye, Shannon." He slowly walked from the house into the dark night. He shivered, but not from the cold.

Bruce walked down the path to the white fence,

feeling Shannon's eyes watching him from the door-way.

"I hope you find it soon," she called softly and then he heard the door close.

Maybe this time he would.

Chapter 6

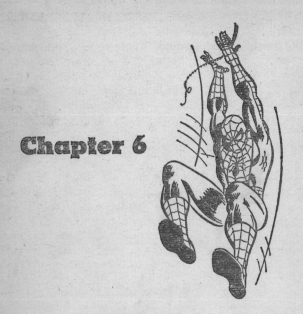

"WHERE THE HELL IS PARKER, MS. Grant!" demanded J. Jonah Jameson.

Glory Grant, the *Daily Bugle*'s red-faced publisher's secretary, looked up from her typing. "How would *I* know, Mr. Jameson? I am not my Parker's keeper."

"That kid could use a keeper," Jameson grumbled. "He's just so typical of the kids these days. Snotty, arrogant, disrespectful. They don't teach them manners like they did when *I* was a kid. It's all that troublemaker Dr. Spock's fault." He chewed thoughtfully on the ragged stump of his cigar. "Remind me to write a personal editorial on that, Ms. Grant. It's a subject that just cries out for the old Jameson flair."

The attractive black girl nodded and wrote "time for annual juvenile-delinquency editorial" on her pad. "You got it, boss."

Jameson headed for his office at the rear of the

large, open city room. "I want to see that punk shutterbug the second he drags his goldbricking butt into the building," he shouted over his shoulder. "And get Tim Coswell from Science down here."

"Yessir!" Glory snapped to attention and saluted Jameson's back. Her hand moved down from her forehead and her thumb touched her nose. She wiggled her fingers at her boss and stuck out her tongue. "You old slave driver, you," she mumbled as his door slammed shut.

Glory Grant sighed and returned to work. She picked up the phone and dialed Peter Parker's number. It was still before noon so it was possible that the young photographer was still asleep, but the phone rang half a dozen times without an answer before she hung up. Peter was probably on his way in.

Next she called Tim Coswell, the *Bugle*'s science editor. The young reporter was surprised and nervous at receiving a summons from the paper's publisher and he told Glory he would be right down. As she was replacing the receiver, she looked across the bustling city room and saw Peter Parker, camera bag slung over his shoulder, whistling happily toward her.

"Good morning, Ms. Grant," he said brightly as he plopped down on the edge of her desk.

"Peter, m'man!" Glory exclaimed. "Why, we'd just about given you up for lost."

"Now, now," he said. "There's a whole lot of that slippery white stuff out there; I think they call it snow. You wouldn't want me to walk too fast and slip, would you? I could get hurt."

"You may get hurt *anyway*," she said, pointing over her shoulder at Jameson's office. "If you catch my drift."

"Is that a snow joke?"

"Yeah. You think I'm *shoveling* it on too much?"

"Well, your sense of humor's not gonna set the city room off on a *flurry* of laughter."

"Enough!" Glory shrieked. "One more pun and I

swear I'll beat myself to death with a rubber chicken!"

Peter jumped to his feet. "Right! Besides, the lion awaits this poor Daniel in his den."

"You were scheduled to be eaten fifteen minutes ago, Daniel," she grinned. "And the lion's gettin' hungrier every second you waste out here."

Peter flinched. "Gotcha. See you later, Glory."

"Good luck, Daniel."

Peter pushed open the door to the inner office. *I really need this? After playing superhero and ace news photographer all night, I still had to spend a couple of hours with the physics books. Then, after two whole hours of sleep, I spend the better part of the morning filling out little blue examination booklets with theories and calculations I'm still not sure I understand.*

And now, to top it all off, I gotta worry about Jameson when he's ticked off at me. Thank goodness I've had plenty of practice at it. Jolly Jonah's never not angry at me!

"Where've you been, Parker?" Jameson barked in greeting. The grizzled newspaper publisher was seated behind his desk, puffing angry clouds of blue smoke into the air around his head.

"All kinds of places," Peter grinned.

"Don't mouth off to me, kid. You almost missed the damn boat," Jameson growled.

Peter looked at his boss, confused. "If not the boat, at least your point. What boat are you referring to?"

"The navy ship." Jameson jabbed a finger at the buttons on his intercom. "Ms. Grant," he bellowed.

"He's coming now, Mr. Jameson," she barked back.

"What navy? Which ship? Who's coming?" Peter scratched his head. "Where am I?"

"I wonder about that myself sometimes," Jameson said.

There was a hesitant knock at the door.

"Come in, damn it!"

The door opened and Tim Coswell stuck his head

in. "Er, Mr. Jameson," he said, clearing his throat. "You wanted to see . . ."

Jameson frowned in annoyance and waved the tall, blond man in. "Not wanted, Coswell. *Had* to. What do you know about StarLab I?"

Coswell stepped inside and gently closed the door. He reached up and pushed his wire-framed glasses up the bridge of his nose. "Oh, well . . . ah, StarLab . . ."

"Don't you know?" Jameson growled, leaning forward in his chair to fix a cold stare on the nervous man. "I mean, we *do* pay you to edit the science section, don't we, Mr. Coswell?"

Coswell blushed and nervously chewed on his lower lip. "Yessir," he said, his voice cracking. He cleared his throat again. "Of course I know . . . ah, I know about StarLab . . . sir. Mr. Jameson."

"Then why the hell aren't you telling us about it?" Jameson yelled.

The nervous science editor flushed even deeper.

Hooboy! Jameson's really got this one cowed. I suppose it is my duty as a fellow cowee to jump in and lend the poor slob a helping hand.

"Isn't that the satellite that's supposed to be falling from its orbit?" Peter asked Jameson.

"Yes!" Coswell nodded almost convulsively, flashing the young photographer a look of gratitude. "Yes," he repeated, seeming to compose himself. "NASA sent StarLab into orbit three years ago as their first step in establishing orbiting space stations. It was inhabited by three separate crews of three for about a year and a half. It's been circling the Earth, its systems shut down, since then.

"About six months ago, NASA noticed that StarLab's orbit was decaying." He glanced over at Jameson. "That's when an orbiting body in space, so close to the planet that it never completely escapes its gravitational influence, is pulled closer and closer with each orbit by the drag of the upper atmosphere until it finally hits the atmosphere in an uncontrolled reentry. In theory, the object burns up in reentry."

"I *know* that," Jameson snarled with contempt.

"Oh, right," Coswell agreed, nodding quickly. He hurried on, "Anyway, they tried correcting the satellite's orbit with small maneuvering jets on board, but that was only a temporary solution. Those jets didn't have enough power or fuel to do the job and prevent an uncontrolled reentry. And when that does happen, it could be big trouble for NASA and some select portion of the world."

"Why? Does somebody, somewhere collect rent on the place?" Peter asked. He fiddled restlessly with the zipper on his camera case.

Coswell started to giggle but caught himself before Jameson noticed. "Ahem. No, Peter," he said. "You see, small objects will burn up completely in reentry, but larger things, especially something the size of Star-Lab, won't. Part of it will burn, but a large part of those 100 tons will make it through.

"And it's got to fall *somewhere!*"

Peter nodded.

"Remember what happened in Canada in 1978 when that Soviet satellite crashed there. They were lucky that it fell in an unpopulated area, but there was still the problem of the nuclear materials used to power the satellite contaminating the area with radiation. It's the same thing in this case, especially since several of StarLab's experimental and equipment packages contain nuclear isotopes."

"That's all real interesting," Peter said. "But you'll pardon me if I ask so what? What am I supposed to do, take pictures of Tim telling us about it?"

"No, wiseass," Jameson snapped. "The thing's coming down and you're supposed to take pictures of the navy catching it."

Peter smiled in sudden understanding. "Ohh, *that* navy ship."

"If you'd pay attention once in a while instead of flapping your gums all the time you'd have heard me say that, Parker," Jameson said. "NASA can't keep their blasted tin can up there any longer and they figure it'll come down early tomorrow morning."

"Where?"

"That they *haven't* figured yet. You'd think with all of the money they waste on their blasted computers they'd know where a stupid hunk of tin was going to fall," the *Bugle* publisher grumbled. "They say it'll either be somewhere in Asia or a couple of hundred miles due east of here in the Atlantic. Damned eggheads!"

"That narrows it down," Coswell muttered.

"It becomes clear to me now, Tim," Peter said, rising to his feet. "You and I have drawn sea duty."

"That's almost intelligent, Parker," Jameson said, spitting the soggy stump of his cigar into the wastebasket by his desk. "The aircraft carrier USS *Alexander Hamilton* is docked at the Port of Jersey in Newark. You two have just enough time to get there before she sets sail."

Coswell blinked. "B . . . but, Mr. Jameson, sir—my wife . . ."

"You can't take your wife on a blasted aircraft carrier," Jameson mumbled absently around a fresh cigar.

"No, I . . . I mean, she's expecting . . . how long will we, ah, be . . . away, sir?" the young science editor stuttered.

"Not at all," Jameson said glancing up angrily. "If you don't get the lead out and make that ship, Coswell. Ms. Grant has your press passes."

"Hope you won't miss me while I'm gone, Mr. J.," Peter smiled.

"I'd miss cholera faster than I'd miss you, Parker." The *Bugle*'s publisher rose, glaring at the smiling young photographer. "Now, *out!*" he bellowed.

Peter grabbed Coswell's arm and pulled him toward the door. "C'mon, Tim," he said. "There's just no talking to the man when he gets this way."

Chapter 7

THE MASSIVE DECK OF THE AIRCRAFT carrier USS *Alexander Hamilton* was uncharacteristically alive with activity two hours before dawn. Uniformed seamen manned their stations across the length of the great warship, its decks alone larger than several football fields laid end to end. Jet helicopters landed and took off continually at the vessel's fore, sweeping off into the sea of darkness that surrounded the brightly lit ship cutting through the frothy swells of the cold Atlantic Ocean.

Peter Parker and Tim Coswell stood huddled in the salty cold of the ship's bridge, leaning against a railing as they watched the activity below. Despite the warmth of the clothes they wore, both men shivered slightly in the cold sea air.

"I wish they'd get on with it," Coswell said through chattering teeth. "I don't think I can take much more of this cold."

Peter unslung his camera from his shoulder and

pointed it at the deck. He began to idly snap photographs of the men and machines being moved around below. "These things take time," he sighed. He clicked off a shot of a sailor signaling a chopper in for a landing. "According to the last announcement, Star-Lab should be passing over us in its next orbit in a few minutes." His telephoto lens caught a sailor in mid leap from the cockpit of a bulky cargo copter.

Coswell rubbed his hands together. "Yeah, well, you don't have to worry about filing a good story with Jameson. *I* do," he said miserably. "Jeez, I don't know what the man's got against me all of a sudden, but . . ."

"What makes you think Jameson's got something against you?"

"Come on, Peter," Tim Coswell said glumly. "You saw the way he tore into me yesterday, didn't you? Hell, I can't figure it. I don't think I've spoken two words to the man in my whole life before he called me into his office."

Peter slapped the unhappy reporter on the back. "Hey, if that's all that's worrying you, friend," he smiled, "don't. It ain't you, believe me. Smiling Jonah Jameson hates *everybody*."

"Yeah, sure," Coswell said, unconvinced. He turned to look at Peter. "If he hates everybody, what about you?"

Peter poked a finger in his chest, looking surprised. "*Me?* What've I got to do with the price of hostile newspaper publishers?"

"C'mon," he said. "I see the way you stand up to him in the city room all the time. You're not afraid of Jameson."

Peter laughed. "Boy, have you got the wrong number, man. I like to think that about the only people J.J. Jameson likes less than me are Santa Claus, the Easter Bunny, and Spider-Man." He brought his camera to his eye. "True, Jameson doesn't scare me, but then I've been known to take midnight strolls along the waterfront, so you can't go by me."

Coswell grinned. "The Easter Bunny?"

The young photographer shrugged. "I know. Sometimes it's really tough to judge a man."

A series of shrill whistles pierced the silence. Peter looked into the bridge housing and saw the white-uniformed captain standing in the dull-green light cast by the radar screens. *At last! Something's finally going to happen. Coswell's a nice guy, salt of the Earth and all that stuff, but I've been playing Dear Abby to his "Miserable In New York Journalism" since yesterday morning and frankly, enough is enough.*

"Attention!" the captain said into a microphone, relaying his words throughout the ship on the public-address system. The sailors stopped what they were doing and waited. "NASA Houston tracking station reports StarLab I has left orbit and is in reentry stage. Trajectory and radar reports show her to be headed straight into our laps, men. Let's get ready."

A cheer arose from the assemblage below and even before it faded, the seamen were all running to their appointed tasks. A large, hydraulically operated platform rose from the belly of the great ship, bringing more helicopters up to the deck. A few took off immediately, veering off into the slowly lightening morning sky.

Coswell excitedly nudged Peter with his elbow. "It's almost time," he said enthusiastically, the prospect of the excitement to come making the blond science editor forget his worries.

Peter, in the middle of trying to change the lens on his camera when the animated jostling began, scowled. "Yeah," he mumbled.

"We have StarLab I on our screens," the captain announced.

The young photographer squinted into the darkness, but it was impossible to see beyond the glare of the carrier's lights.

"StarLab coordinates, altitude 98 knots, downrange 11 knots, west."

"Ready, Peter?" Coswell had to shout to make himself heard above the deafening roar of the choppers.

Peter flashed his companion the okay sign.

"Altitude 85 knots, downrange 9 kn . . ." Without a sound, the public-address system went dead.

Peter and Coswell looked at each other simultaneously.

"Think maybe somebody cut the strings on their tin cans?" Peter asked after several seconds of silence.

Coswell shook his head. "I don't know," he said. "Maybe something went wrong with StarLab?"

"What could go wrong? It was up there and it was falling to here. It's *got* to come down."

"But what if it wasn't . . . ?"

"Then I guess Isaac Newton was just playing a big joke on everybody with all that 'what goes up must come down' jive." Peter stared ahead into the sky, frowning. "Still, they should have said something by now." He looked over his shoulder into the bridge housing. The captain was no longer standing talking into a microphone. He was across the cabin shouting frantically into a telephone handset and pointing wildly at the radar. *Something is most definitely not kosher in Denmark.*

Activity on the deck had all but stopped. The men stood in small confused groups, looking to the PA speakers for further orders. What was happening on the bridge could only be speculated upon in low murmurs by the bewildered sailors. For almost two minutes, there was nothing and then, "Attention, all hands! Operations reports a change in scheduling. We will maintain present position until signaled. That is all."

No it ain't, brother!

Change of plans, huh? I wonder how they plan to put about twenty-five tons of red hot, falling scrap metal on hold! And seeing as they're not about to tell us anything until it's too late to do any good—and besides, I'm just too goshdarned nosy to wait—I think it's time for me to take a little moonlight stroll around the deck and find out.

Spidey style!

Peter turned to Coswell. "Listen, Tim," he murmured conspiratorially. "I think the navy's trying to put something over on us."

"Yeah?"

"Oh, yeah. Why else don't they say anything?"

Tim Coswell considered this for several seconds. "Yeah," he said slowly. "I think you might be right, Peter."

"We ought to check it out, don't you think?"

"Well . . . I dunno. What d'you think?"

"Hey, I'm only the photographer around here, Tim. As the reporter on the scene, *you,* as we say in the darkroom, call the shots and *I* just take 'em." Peter looked around as if making certain they were not being overheard. "But since you ask, I think we should. Think of what breaking a story like this could mean to your career."

"Yeah!" Coswell pounded his fist into his hand. "Okay, let's go, Peter!"

"Um, don't you think we'd cover a lot more ground if we split up?" Peter asked as he started backing slowly away from the young science editor. "Y'know, talk to the sailors, officers, NASA people, like that."

"Right!" Coswell's face was set in a look of determination as he hurried to the ladder leading to the deck below.

Peter smiled at the retreating man's back. *Jeez, I probably could have sold him the Brooklyn Bridge just now if I'd wanted to. Tim's just lucky I left the ownership papers in my other pair of pants today.*

Checking to make sure he was alone on the dark bridge, Peter walked briskly around to the other side of the deck. He kept close to the cold, damp bulkhead, ducking beneath open portholes to avoid detection. When he was safely in the shadows and away from accidental probing eyes, he stooped and quickly removed his shoes. Then, glancing around a final time, Peter Parker started climbing up the steel wall.

The young photographer had spied an open porthole at the rear of the large cabin housing the ship's bridge. It faced the open sea and a narrow walkway ran beneath it, shielding that section of the wheelhouse from view from below. Peter scampered up the wall and then cut across the top of the wall until he came to the small, open porthole located not two yards behind the captain's back.

Peter clung flat against the bulkhead, making certain his body was well hidden in shadows. He hung over the small circle of light in the dark metal. *I wonder if Woodward and Bernstein got started this way?*

Inside, the captain was on the telephone, speaking anxiously to somewhere on the mainland while he stood over the green-lit radar screens. "Yessir," he was saying. His face was tight with anxiety. "I fully realize NASA's position in the situation, but . . ." He stopped, listening for long moments while impatiently drumming his fingers on the console before him. "No, sir," he said quickly. "We've checked, rechecked, and *re*-rechecked all the equipment. It's operating at peak efficiency. What does NASA get on their screens?" He took his cap off, scratched his head and replaced it. "Uh-huh."

The captain let out a long sigh of resignation. "Then what can *I* tell you, sir? The *Hamilton,* the *Portsmith,* and even NASA say the same thing and I seriously doubt that all our equipment would go out in the same way at the same time."

The agitated commander stared out a window at the rising sun. "Then I'm afraid we're just going to have to face it, sir," he said firmly. "Somehow, someway, StarLab I has disappeared out from under our noses!"

And despite himself, Peter Parker whistled in amazement from his hiding place outside the cabin window. It was several seconds later that he realized his spider-sense had begun to tingle ferociously at the captain's words.

Chapter 8

"SNOW, SNOW AND *more* DAMNED snow!" snarled the burly man sitting hunched behind the wheel of the tractor trailer, peering hopelessly through the white-blanketed windshield.

Bruce Banner started and sat up sharply. The man's angry mutterings had roused him from the light, uneasy sleep he had been drifting in and out of for the past several hours. Despite the comfortable warmth of the truck cab, Bruce was sweating heavily—the cold, clammy sweat of fear. He blinked and looked around, wondering what could have brought about his fear.

Then he remembered.

He had been dreaming—vague, shimmering visions of emerald-colored rage that seemed to have grown into a constant, horrifying companion to his every sleeping hour. In his nightmares, the young scientist was but a spectator standing on the sidelines of a brilliant green scene, watching in undisguised horror and

70

revulsion the uncontrollable fury that was himself. The man-monster loped through the glistening fog, caught in a seemingly endless dance of mindless, wanton destruction.

Gigantic tanks rolled toward him, only to be reduced to piles of twisted wreckage by battering emerald fists.

Helicopters, distorted by nightmare, flew overhead to be smashed into falling debris.

Jet fighters with hideous, flapping wings of metallic feathers swept through the sky, exploding into nova-bright balls of flame when struck by a missile of radiation-mutated flesh and sinew.

Death was a heavy stink in the air.

But Bruce Banner could only stand and watch, unable to move, to escape the rampaging engine of destruction that drew closer to the young scientist with each swipe of its sledgehammer fists. He was trapped, held as if by an invisible web, awaiting his end at the mercy of the giant spider that spun it.

The creature drew closer, its features swirling about its face in an unrecognizable mass of jade. But the features started taking shape before Banner now. He stared in horror, his mouth opened to scream a scream that would not come from his dry throat.

Blank, lifeless eyes stared from beneath the creature's hideous, protruding brow at the shivering scientist.

Bruce Banner recognized the eyes . . . that face. . . .

And only then could he scream.

The face of death was his own!

"I says are ya awright, fella?"

Bruce blinked rapidly, drawing a shaking hand across his clammy forehead. It's all right, he told himself. He was safe. The creature was far, far away.

"And always with me," he murmured, unaware he had spoken aloud.

The burly driver tore his eyes off the snow-covered road and glanced at the pale young man seated next to him. "You ain't sick or nothin', are ya?" he asked.

"Jeez, I hope ya ain't sick. It ain't that I wouldn't wanna help youse or nothin' like that, but, Jeez, with this weather, I'm awready a half a day behind schedule and if I don't get these ballbearin's to Toledo on time . . ."

Bruce wearily shook his head. "No," he said softly. "I'm fine. Really."

The driver turned back to the road, cursing the slow, snarled traffic along Chicago's Edens Expressway. "'At's good, 'cause I just ain't got the time to help youse now." He made an angry gesture at the road. "I mean, willya lookit that, for cryin' out loud. You think they'd do somethin', y'know. Plow. Salt. Somethin'! But, nah, they ain't gotta drive in this crud. . . ."

Bruce tuned out the driver's angry mutterings and stared silently out the side window. It had been nearly two days since he had left MacDermont Point, hitching rides along the way that finally led him into the nearly snowbound city of Chicago and his destination. The snow had started in the Windy City early yesterday evening and had continued unabated throughout the night and into the morning. Thirteen inches of snow buried the city now.

The young scientist could see nothing through the steadily falling curtain of snowflakes. It was day, he knew, but only because a clock on the dashboard told him so.

"Where are we?" Bruce asked, interrupting the driver's running commentary.

"Messed up, that's where we are," the man grumbled. "What, you think I *wanna* go this way, like it don't add an extra hun'red miles to the trip goin' through the city? But they're closin' all th' highways 'cause o' the . . ."

"What I meant was, are we in Chicago yet?"

"Chi? Hell, yeah," the man laughed. "What'cha think we been ridin' through the past couple o' miles? Hoboken?" He laughed again at his own joke. "Heh,

Hoboken." He jerked his thumb to the east. "Lake Whatchamacallit—Michigan is over that way."

Bruce nodded even though he couldn't see a thing.

"Lookit, buddy, I'm gonna be pullin' off o' the expressway and try'n ta cut through the city. You got any place in particular ya wanna be dropped?"

"LaSalle Street," Bruce said. "823 LaSalle Street. Do you know where that is?"

The driver laughed and reached over and punched Bruce lightly on the arm. "Do *I* know Chi? You kiddin' me? I spent six months here durin' the war, y'know." He smiled in fond remembrance. "Yeah, the war was great. Yeah, now, lemme see. 823 LaSalle's right over by Water Tower Place, right?"

"I'll have to take your word for it. This is my first time in Chicago."

"Well, you sure picked a helluva time to come visitin'." The driver slapped his hand down hard on the steering wheel. "I mean, ya ever see snow like this? Not in New York or Boston or Philly, nope. But Chicago, Jeez, it's *always* snowin' in Chicago."

The burly man turned all his attention to his driving, concentrating on pulling his tractor trailer off the highway through the stalled morning traffic and snowdrifts without serious mishap. Half an hour later, after a trip which normally took ten minutes, the driver pulled his rig over to the curb on Chicago Avenue.

"Last stop," he called as he jammed the gearshift into neutral.

Bruce Banner reached over and shook the other man's hand. "Thanks a lot, friend," he said. "I really appreciate the ride."

The burly man dismissed Bruce's thanks with a wave of his hand. "Aw, don't mention it, buddy. Glad to have the company. And take it easy out there," he warned. "The wind's kickin' up somethin' fierce."

"Will do." Bruce opened the door and jumped from the warm cab into over a foot of powdery snow. He waved to the man behind the wheel before turning and starting off through the raging storm.

The young scientist hunched his shoulders against the battering wind that whipped off the lake. He tied his hood tightly around his head. The wind churned the snow into swirling whirlwinds that piled into high drifts against the sides of buildings, parked cars, and anything else that did not move. And the snow continued to fall, adding over an inch an hour to the heavy accumulation already on the ground. Bruce could not see more than a few feet in front of him.

He hurried east on Chicago Avenue, then south on deserted LaSalle Street. 823 was not far away.

"May I help you, sir?"

Bruce Banner brushed the melting flakes of snow from his coat. "Yes," he said to the pretty young receptionist seated in the waiting room of the Institute for Radiation Research's modern plastic-and-chrome office. "I'd like to see Dr. Irvine if he's in."

The raven-haired girl smiled. "Do you have an appointment with the doctor?" she asked, reaching for the telephone on her desk.

"No, I don't."

"Oh, well, then I'm sorry, sir, but the doctor is very busy. . . ."

Bruce rubbed his red, chapped hands together, a look of alarm spreading across his handsome features. "Please, miss," he said. "I . . . I've just come into town and it's extremely urgent I speak with Dr. Irvine. It's about his research. Please."

"Well . . ." The girl chewed thoughtfully on her lip, looking at the distraught man in front of her desk. She lifted the phone. "I guess it wouldn't hurt to *ask*, would it?"

Bruce breathed a sigh of relief. "Thank you."

"Doctor?" she said into the phone, "there's a gentleman here to see you. . . . Yes, I told him, Dr. Irvine, but he insists it's important." She looked up. "May I have your name, please."

"Banner. Dr. Bruce Banner."

She repeated his name into the phone and nodded.

"Very good, Doctor," she said and hung up. "Dr. Irvine will be right out, Dr. Banner. Will you have a seat?"

Bruce sat down.

Soon, he told himself. Soon.

"Can I get you a cup of coffee, Doctor?" the receptionist asked.

"Yes, please," Bruce smiled at her. He hadn't realized how much he could use one.

The girl got up and disappeared through a side door leading to the inner office.

A moment later another door opened and a tall, gray-haired man in a white lab coat entered the reception area. "Dr. Banner," he said enthusiastically as he extended his hand.

Bruce jumped to his feet. "Yes. Dr. Irvine?"

The older man nodded, shaking Bruce's hand. "It's a great honor to meet you, Dr. Banner," he smiled broadly. "A great honor indeed. I'm what you might call," he chuckled briefly, "quite a fan of your papers and books. And, of course, I've heard a great deal about you over the years."

"I'm sure," Bruce said, laughing bitterly.

Dr. Irvine shook his head in sympathy. "Yes," he said, "a terrible thing, that accident of yours. It's a miracle you were able to survive such a massive dose of gamma radiation—far more than any man I've come across in all my years of research."

"I suppose it does make me pretty much an oddity," Bruce admitted.

"Oh, no, Doctor," Irvine said quickly. "Not an oddity, a *victim*. But a victim of a disease that now, fortunately, has a cure."

Bruce nodded. "I read of your work here at the institute. The papers reported you had discovered a means of reversing the effects of gamma radiation."

Dr. Irvine nodded.

"Then it's true?"

"Indeed we have." the scientist said proudly. "Of course, we're still running a few tests on our findings, but I feel safe in saying that my conclusions will be borne out one hundred percent."

"I know. And I'd like to volunteer my services to the institute. As a guinea pig and a scientist."

"Why," Dr. Irvine seemed pleasantly stunned, "we would be honored to have you on the staff, Dr. Banner. Your early research into gamma radiation was the basic foundation for all our work here."

"And my . . . condition? Can your cure help me?"

"The Hulk?" Dr. Irvine smiled. "As I understand it, the gamma-bomb explosion you were caught in irradiated your body's cell structure with a lethal dose of gamma rays, correct? But instead of causing death, the radiation caused a freak mutation that triggers the metamorphosis.

"We've had success eliminating excess radiation in test animals with similar, albeit less intense cases of gamma poisoning in the past. . . ." The doctor paused and squinted past Banner, thoughtfully stroking his chin.

Without realizing it, Bruce held his breath.

"Frankly, Dr. Banner, I can't think of any reason why your particular problem can't be dealt with as easily as those other cases."

Bruce Banner exhaled sharply. Suddenly, it felt as if a great weight had been lifted from his frail shoulders. A great, green weight of rampaging hatred. He laughed aloud, a natural enough reaction that the young scientist had not genuinely experienced in many long years.

"Then what are we waiting for, Dr. Irvine? Let's get started."

The secretary walked back into the room carrying a paper cup full of coffee. "Here we are, Dr. Banner," she said pleasantly.

"Ah, Miss Winters," Irvine said. "The good doctor has graciously consented to join our staff. I'm sure he's most anxious to tour the facilities and begin work. So if you would please call the airport and have them ready our plane for immediate use."

She handed Bruce the coffee with a smile and returned to her desk and the telephone.

"Airport?" Bruce was confused.

"Oh, I'm so sorry, Dr. Banner," Irvine said. "I forgot to tell you. This is only one of several of the institute's regional offices around the country. Our main research facility is located in upstate New York, just outside the city of Niagara Falls." The scientist frowned. "I hope there's nothing keeping you here?"

"There hasn't been much of anything holding me anywhere for a long time, Doctor. That's why I'm here. To change that."

Bruce took a sip of the hot, black coffee while Dr. Irvine went into the inner office to prepare for the trip. The coffee tasted good. But then, everything was good.

Now.

Chapter 9

CHICAGO'S O'HARE FIELD HAS THE reputation for being the world's busiest airport. Each day, at this sprawling airfield some fifteen miles from downtown Chicago, more airplanes take off and land with more passengers than at any other airport on Earth.

But as far as Bruce Banner could tell, squeezed uncomfortably between Dr. Irvine and Miss Winters on the front seat of the doctor's Land Rover, O'Hare International was having a tough time living up to its reputation in the middle of the severest snowstorm to hit the midwest in five decades. Onto the seven runways that handled the traffic, snow blew and drifted faster than the exhausted maintenance men could sweep it aside with snowplows. The few flights cleared for takeoff were forced to wait hours at the end of the single runway that still remained operational. They stood with taxiing lights blinking in the dull-gray day while harried air-traffic controllers sought a hole in the storm through which to send them on their way. All incoming flights had been diverted to other airports outside the area of the blizzard that held the Great Lakes region in its icy grasp. Most airlines had canceled many of their flights, stranding in the terminals untold thousands of disgruntled passengers, unable to find either transportation into the city or rooms in the airport's packed hotels.

Soon, O'Hare International Airport would be forced to close for only the third time in its existence.

"Are you sure we'll be able to get a flight out of here?" Bruce asked uncertainly.

Dr. Irvine kept his eyes on the snow-covered road as he maneuvered around cars stalled in the deep drifts. "Not if we were relying on the airlines," he said. "But the institute maintains its own private plane. Ahh, here we are."

The doctor stopped the four-wheel drive vehicle in front of the main terminal and switched off the ignition. "No sense trying to fight our way into one of the parking lots," he said. "Of course, our plane isn't as big or as comfortable as a 747, nor does it offer much in the way of stewardesses," he smiled, "but it will get us where we want to go. Shall we?"

Dr. Irvine, Bruce, and Miss Winters piled out of the jeep and hurried into the main terminal.

There were people everywhere; men, women, and children filled the relatively few seats; the remainder of the people huddled in groups on the floor with their luggage. Outraged passengers crowded a dozen deep at the reservation counters, demanding the airlines end the storm and ship them off to their destinations.

The trio weaved through the crowd, heading toward the rear of the terminal, just three more stranded, anonymous travelers among the tens of thousands there.

"*Dr. Banner!*"

The shout was heard by Bruce over the subdued

murmur of the disgruntled throng. He stopped and looked around, his brow creased in puzzlement. He knew no one in Chicago. . . .

"Dr. Banner, please," Irvine said, pushing him gently forward. "We still have a chance to fly out before they close the airport—*if* we hurry."

Bruce nodded. "I thought I heard . . ."

"Banner!"

The young scientist saw the man shouting his name now as the man pushed his way rudely through the crowd with others following close behind. The handsome young man wore a blazer with one of the television network's logos stitched on the breast pocket and held a microphone in his outstretched hand. The mike was attached by a long wire to the hand-held miniature camera hoisted on the shoulder of the man behind him. Several of the others in the advancing group also held minicams or still cameras.

"Reporters!" Irvine hissed angrily.

"What are they doing here?" Bruce asked quickly.

"Probably reporting on the blizzard," Miss Winters said.

Bruce felt his pulse begin to race. "I . . . I'd rather not have to talk to them."

"Of course, my boy," Irvine said. "I completely understand." He glanced around and pointed to a closed door just beyond the empty baggage-claim area several yards to their right. The door was marked AUTHORIZED PERSONNEL ONLY BEYOND THIS POINT. "Perhaps we can lose them in there."

They started for the door, but the reporters, all expert in cornering unwilling subjects for interviews, intercepted them. Bright lights were flicked on and shone in the agitated young scientist's face as eager reporters thrust their microphones at him.

"Dr. Banner . . ."

"Could you comment on . . ."

". . . the army says you . . ."

". . . the Hulk demolished a special task force. Is that . . ."

". . . true, Dr. Banner?"

"The New Mexican authorities . . ."

". . . comment, Dr. Banner . . ."

"Please," Bruce pleaded. "No comment—I . . ."

He felt his chest tighten and he was gasping for breath. His heart was pounding and the blood seemed to rush to his head. He was dizzy. He tried to blink away the blinding lights, but they stayed on him. The reporters, clinging like leeches, would not go away, would not stop their incessant shouting.

"Leave me . . . alone . . ." he pleaded. The blood was pounding in his ears like a drum.

It was happening!

"What're you doing in Chicago, Dr. Banner?"

"Can you comment on the army's report?"

"Has the Hulk . . ."

"Leave me alone!" the frail scientist screamed suddenly.

The world shimmered before his eyes, an emerald haze that clouded his world. He hunched over suddenly as if in great pain and the cluster of reporters closed in on him.

The last thing Dr. Bruce Banner remembered as he crumpled to the floor was the sharp tearing of cloth, for, when he rose to his feet a moment later, he was no longer the small, frail scientist.

He was the Hulk!

Chapter 10

TWO MEN, CLAD IN BULKY, WHITE protective gear stepped from the larger chamber into the smaller room adjoining it. They carefully sealed the heavy steel door behind them before peeling off the oversized jump suits they wore and disposing of them in a chute set into the airlock's wall. The suits, however, were not worn to protect these crew-cutted technicians from any hazard within the chamber; rather they were to guard the thing that rested inside from any risk of contamination from outside. Nothing that had not first been sterilized entered the heavily protected chamber, not a man, not even the pencil he wrote with. Even the air flowed through six separate filters and processing units before it was allowed to be pumped inside.

The delicate instrument assembled inside the chamber was not built to withstand any other conditions on Earth, for a single speck of dust inside one of the microscopically tuned and calibrated mechanisms could sharply reduce its amazing accuracy and efficiency.

Now wearing plain, unmarked jump suits, the two men left the small airlock and entered a vast low-ceilinged room lined with neat rows of computer terminals, each manned by a similarly dressed technician. Each man or woman wore headphone and microphone sets and was busily working at their keyboard and readout screen, entering complex data and testing various systems. Set in the wall at the front of the room was a large plate-glass window that looked into the chamber beyond the airlock. A lone, long console faced the window and half a dozen men, also wearing headphones, sat behind it. These men, generally older than the technicians, were clad in white shirts and ties, and clean white laboratory smocks. Behind the man in the center of the console stood two other men who watched the scientists work with their arms folded patiently across their chests.

The man at the center console glanced up from his readout screen and flashed the thumbs-up sign to the two technicians. He was an older man with white hair that grew in a wild fringe around his otherwise bald head. Thick framed bifocals were perched on the bridge of his nose and the rest of his face was lost beneath a full, scraggly white beard.

"It's working fine now," he said.

The two men nodded and returned to their desks.

"Well, Prof. Warner?" the taller of the two men behind him asked. He was a slim, handsome man with finely chiseled features and neatly trimmed salt-and-pepper hair. He was impeccably dressed in a dark pin-striped Cardin suit and shiny Gucci loafers. His eyes were a cold, hard gray. His voice relayed unquestionable authority in the subdued atmosphere of the control room.

"We'll begin in a moment, Mr. Pendergast," the scientist said without looking up.

The man named Pendergast nodded and looked into the chamber. There was not much to see inside, just a five foot by five foot square swathed in protective plastic wrapping in front of the window. A small tube protruded from the front of the box.

A conveyor belt hung from the ceiling at the far end of the chamber. Clamps held a foot-thick slab of steel suspended in the air.

Prof. Abraham Warner consulted his computer readout and nodded his satisfaction. "System M ready for testing," he said softly into the microphone. "Stand by."

Warner flipped switches and pressed buttons on the panel before him. Green lights blinked on signaling the system's readiness. Instantly, information flashed across the screen, changing every few seconds as the systems switched on.

"On zero," Warner said and began counting backward from five. When he reached zero he pressed another switch and the plastic-wrapped box began to hum ever so slightly. The lens at the tip of the protruding tube glowed bright red.

The tube swiveled in line with the slab of steel. A pencil-thin beam of ruby-red light flashed from it and struck the steel dead center. Instantly, a hole appeared in the metal.

Warner manipulated the computer keyboard and the lens swiveled around in a complete circle. The center of the slab fell to the floor with a clang, a perfect inch-wide circle of red-hot metal.

The red beam disappeared and the conveyor belt started to move. A second slab of metal rolled into the room. As soon as it appeared, the lens seemed to lock on it, tracking it across the room until a wide beam of red energy flashed from it.

The second metal slab disintegrated.

Steel plates continued to roll by the black box and its deadly beam that blasted, melted, and shattered the heavy metal. One plate, with a series of fifty almost-microscopic sensors implanted in it, was blasted in perfect sequence by the beam in a span of less than two seconds.

Pendergast nodded approvingly as he watched the demonstration. The short squat man dressed in a black suit behind him stared in rapt fascination. "Amazing," he whispered to the taller man.

"It is, isn't it," Pendergast smiled. "And this is merely the device's secondary function. Quite a neat little toy, wouldn't you say, Lloyd?"

"Yessir, Mr. Pendergast," Lloyd replied.

Prof. Warner switched off his device and turned to the tall man and his assistant. "Well, Mr. Pendergast?" the aged scientist asked.

"Very impressive, Prof. Warner," the man said. "Now if the main mode is operating as well, I would say we were well on our way."

"It is," Warner assured him. "The microwave transceiver is ready to be put into immediate operation as soon as the delivery vehicle is completed."

Pendergast glanced at his watch. "Then it should be very soon, Prof. Warner," he said. "Even now, the remaining hardware we need is safely hidden away and should be in our hands within the next twenty-four hours.

"And once we have StarLab, Doctor, our waiting will be over!"

Chapter 11

"Hulk said men better leave Hulk alone!"

The giant green man-brute roared as awareness came to him. The Hulk was bewildered by the strange surroundings and angered by the thousands of people who seemed to be closing in around him in the O'Hare Airport terminal.

He flung his thick emerald arms to his sides, swatting aside those reporters not swift enough to avoid him. Frightened, the other newsmen backed slowly away, but their instincts for a story pretty much overcame their fear of the man-monster. They held their ground. Photographers snapped pictures and minicam operators kept their video cameras rolling while anxious newsmen whispered tense, hurried commentary into microphones.

The Hulk crouched with his wide jade back pressed against the wall. His dull-green eyes shifted constantly beneath his protruding brow, watching the reporters with the look of a wild cornered beast.

His lips turned up at the corners when he spotted the cameras. "Stupid-looking guns won't stop Hulk," he growled menacingly. "*Nothing* puny men have can stop Hulk."

The jade giant ambled forward, pulling the tattered remains of Bruce Banner's new parka from his massive shoulders. The reporters continued shuffling backward, always staying well beyond the man-monster's reach.

Then a woman glimpsed the Hulk through the throng of reporters. Her reaction was extremely typical of a grandmother from Canton, Ohio who sees a giant green monster coming toward her in an airport terminal:

She screamed.

The Hulk started, startled by the sudden piercing screech. But within seconds, others, alerted now to the Hulk's presence, joined in the screaming. They began a mad dash away from the green-skinned behemoth, running in a blind panic that swiftly turned the thousands of individuals into a single, mindless mob.

"That's right," the Hulk bellowed after them. "Run! Puny people better run from Hulk because Hulk can *smash* you all! Hulk can smash anything!"

He squatted and then sprang up toward the ceiling. His emerald fists crashed through the reinforced concrete ceiling. The Hulk pulled himself up to the second level, seeking escape from the screaming, fleeing mob.

But the upper floor was as crowded as the floor below, thus insuring the man-monster's spectacular arrival a large audience. Startled passengers gaped in astonishment as the floor buckled beneath their feet and split open with a geyser of dust-and-concrete debris. Great green hands grasped either side of the hole and the muscle-bound body of the Hulk shot up through it.

He saw still more people and roared in anger.

There never seemed to be any escape from them. Everywhere the Hulk went, people waited to hound him. All he desired was freedom and solitude. All they gave him was hatred and an abundance of their number that he could never escape from.

The Hulk loped off in search of that freedom.

To the jade-hued colossus, the O'Hare terminal seemed to be one continuous maze from which there was no way out. He bounded past the baggage-check-in area, his battering fists scattering large piles of luggage that stood in his path. Airline personnel and passengers alike ran for cover. One man dove for a phone beneath his counter and called for help.

But the Hulk continued on, seeking any way out of the terminal.

Three Chicago policemen stood by the corridor to the boarding gates, unaware of the rampaging creature of chaos that loped toward them.

"Think it's ever going to let up, Sarge?" Patrolman Ron Franks asked, staring tiredly at the masses of people stranded by the storm. Because of the emergency created by the weather and the impossibility of transporting replacements to the field, those officers on duty were forced to stay there until the snow stopped.

"Eventually," Sergeant Barry Polanski yawned.

Patrolman Dave O'Donnell found himself yawning along with the sergeant. "Yeah, well, it can't be soon enough for me. Twenty hours on duty is more than enough for me."

"Uh-huh!" Franks agreed. "I don't know how many more times I can stand explaining to these people that the city of Chicago has absolutely no control over the weather."

"Despite what they try to tell you at City Hall," Franks snickered.

"You want excitement, join the fire department," Polanski said. "You ought to know by now that cops spend ninety-nine percent of their time waiting for something to happen and then writing reports after it does."

Polanski cast an idle glance into the terminal. Slowly he straightened, his hand going to rest on the butt of his holstered gun. "Uh, guys," he said. "I think you're about to find out what it's like the other one percent of the time.

"*Look!*"

The two patrolmen turned as the seven-foot-tall, emerald-green behemoth lumbered into view. The three cops whipped their sidearms from their holsters simultaneously and aimed them at the Hulk.

"Okay, fella," Polanski ordered. "Stop right there and start talking and keep your hands in sight!"

The Hulk growled and continued toward the police.

"I said *stop!*" the sergeant shouted.

Thick muscles rippled smoothly beneath his emerald skin as the Hulk bounded across the floor, his big, broad feet slapping rhythmically on the cold tile.

"Sarge," Franks whispered urgently. "Isn't that . . . ?"

Polanski steadied his gun with his left hand. "Yeah," he nodded.

O'Donnell set his sights on the sweaty green chest and tightened his finger around the trigger. "Wh . . . what d'we do?"

The sergeant glanced at first one man, then the other, and then back at the Hulk. The monster was almost upon them and showed no sign of stopping.

What else was there to do?

Sgt. Polanski opened fire, signaling to the others to do the same.

The bullets flattened against the Hulk's thick hide, as effective as a spitball against a charging rhinoceros. "Bah," the big man spat out in disgust. "Hulk cannot be hurt by guns."

The three officers dived out of the way when they saw their bullets had no effect on the man-creature. The Hulk charged past them and swept down the corridor and through a horrified crowd that pressed against the walls to allow the awesome creature passage.

He barreled into the airport's X-ray security station with the speed of a racing locomotive. The fragile stand collapsed under the assault of gamma-charged muscles and the Hulk was through, scarcely noticing the obstacle he had just demolished.

Up ahead waited more police, alerted by frantic calls from Sgt. Polanski over his walkie-talkie. Their guns were drawn and they stood in a line across the wide corridor between the crowded waiting areas.

"*More* guns?" the brute-man growled. They were no more than a petty annoyance here with their tiny guns. Only when they brought out the bigger, more powerful weapons and flying machines did men become any of the Hulk's concern. But here, now? It was far simpler to avoid them.

The Hulk swerved suddenly to his left and leaped over the counter at a deserted boarding area. It was then that he noticed the far wall was a single, huge observation window that faced the landing field. Through the window he saw the airfield was covered by a thick blanket of snow. Dark shapes dotted with multicolored lights moved through it. An empty, silent Boeing 727 stood by the departure gate, its landing gear buried beneath the snow.

The man-creature's eyes flashed briefly as he saw what lay beyond the window. *There* was his freedom! He stood in the center of the lounge, gazing at the windswept snow outside and a twisted smile formed on his emerald lips. He liked the glistening white powder from the sky. It was cool and refreshing against his skin.

Ka-pow! Ka-pow!

One bullet and then another bounced off the Hulk's back as the police rushed into the lounge, guns blazing.

Grunting with rage, the Hulk turned and grabbed the back of one of the rows of seats and yanked them clear of the bolts holding them to the floor. He raised them over his head.

"Go away!" he cried in warning to the policemen. *Bang! Ka-pow!*

The slugs crumpled against his stomach.

"Hulk warned you!" he roared and heaved the row of seats at the cops, bowling them over like tenpins. Then the man-monster turned, crashed through the window, and leaped to the ground twenty feet below.

The Hulk landed in a shower of shattered safety glass in the deep snow. He inhaled huge lungfuls of the cold, crisp air and growled with satisfaction—a deep throaty growl.

Suddenly, a spotlight pierced the white curtain and landed on the Hulk. He swung his arm up in front of his eyes against the glare and cautiously tried to pinpoint the source of this latest discomfort, even though it did not matter. A discomfort was something to be smashed and done away with. And no matter what it was, the Hulk was the one to smash it.

He heard the muffled roar of a diesel engine moving steadily toward him, bringing the glaring spotlight closer. He lumbered forward, eyes squeezed shut against the light. The Incredible Hulk did not need to see to smash one of man's machines.

The snowplow driver urged his machine forward through the blowing snow. He drove in a straight line toward the giant green behemoth who stood before the terminal building framed in an aura of light. He had heard the desperate calls of the airport security men over the plow's radio and, while headed back to the garage, had spotted the giant man-thing crash onto the field.

His plow would put a stop to that thing once and for all!

He pushed his vehicle to top speed and lowered the plow. The driver smiled briefly when he felt the sharp jolt of his machine connecting with the green behemoth. The plow continued rolling forward, shoving the creature back.

But the man's smile vanished as another jolt shook the heavy tractor and it stopped dead in its tracks. He shouted in fear and surprise as the snowplow was lifted smoothly off the snow-covered tarmac.

The Hulk hefted the many tons of machinery over his head. With a yelp of panic the driver leaped from the cab and landed on the run in the deep snow. He disappeared into the safety of the terminal building.

Snarling, the jade-skinned giant tossed the snowplow aside. It flipped through the air and landed on its back on top of a parked fuel truck.

Bahwhooom!

The truck and tractor exploded in a mushroom cloud of flame and black smoke, lighting the field with a sudden, eerie crimson glow.

The Hulk roared his defiance at the flaming wreckage and bounded away from it. Several vehicles were speeding across the field toward him as fast as the snow allowed. Inside were men armed with nothing more than handguns with which to defend themselves against one of the mightiest forces on Earth.

The four-wheel-drive trucks skidded to a halt in a semicircle before the Hulk. The men leaped from the automobiles with guns in hand and took up their positions, shivering not so much from the brutal cold as from fear.

His breath forming white clouds of vapor in the air, the Hulk stood beneath the wing of the 727.

"Hulk has done nothing to you. Why can't you leave Hulk alone?" the man-brute shouted, his harsh, rumbling voice sounding almost plaintive to the policemen.

"We won't hurt you," one man called back. "Come out and surrender and we promise not to hurt you."

"Bah! You think you can hurt Hulk?"

"We don't want *anybody* hurt, Dr. Banner. . . ."

"Not Banner!" The Hulk's sledgehammerlike hands curled into fists at the mere mention of that hated name. "Little man Banner is not here! Only Hulk is here!"

"Please, Dr. Banner!"

"No . . . more . . . puny . . . Banner!" he roared. His thickly muscled arms lashed out and struck the airplane's landing gear. With a screech of metal, the gear crumpled and the plane toppled to one side with its wing dug into the snow.

"Banner is dead! Now only Hulk lives!

"And Hulk will smash you *all!*"

The man-beast reached over his head, never taking his beady little eyes from the row of headlights before him. His fingers curled around the edge of the wing and, with muscles standing out like thick steel cables on his back and arms, he ripped it from the fuselage.

He twisted at the waist, holding the dismembered wing—dangling engine and all—by the narrowest end; and snapped around. The metal wedge sailed through the air like an enormous boomerang at the Hulk's tormentors. It whooshed toward the semicircle of vehicles and landed directly on top of them. The disbelieving security men barely had enough time to fling themselves out of the way before their trucks were buried under the wing.

But the emerald colossus' rampage had just begun. He had pleaded with them to leave him in peace, but, as always, they had ignored his pleas and attacked. Now it was his turn.

He shambled over to the airplane, now lying toppled over on its side, the remaining wing pointing toward the sky. The Hulk crouched beneath the ruined aircraft and, bracing his broad back against the fuselage, began to slowly straighten. Inch by inch, the plane was lifted from the ground, almost fifty tons supported by the awesome strength of the jade-skinned Goliath. Then, with beads of perspiration standing out on his forehead, the Hulk was standing with one hundred and twenty feet of aircraft balanced on his back.

The Hulk began to walk forward, increasing his speed until he was running toward the terminal. Suddenly he stopped and snapped his body forward, sending the airplane sailing through the air.

Propelled by the most powerful muscles in the world, the plane shot forward and crashed heavily into the glass-walled facade of the squat building. The plane slid inside, screeching to a slow stop with two dozen feet of its nose lodged inside the waiting lounge.

Without pause, he turned, his eyes searching for something else to destroy.

A train of flatbed trailers stood parked against the wall of the terminal alongside the enclosed boarding ramp attached to the plane at the next gate. He bounded over to the baggage truck and grunted his approval. This would do nicely. He lifted the lead car in the chain as a child might pick up a toy.

The emerald-green giant snapped the chain of baggage cars through the air like a giant whip and sent it smashing into the aluminum-sided boarding ramp. It broke through the flimsy alloy and flew out the other side to smash with a deafening crash against the side of the airplane. He pushed against the ramp's oversized tires and rolled it into the plane until the metal accordioned into a flat, ruined mass against the fuselage. He ripped the wreckage free and flung it across the field.

The Hulk began pummeling the parked aircraft, smashing through its thick metal skin and tearing loose large hunks of wires and machinery. He pulled free one large jet engine and shoved it through the plane's underbelly. A wing was pounded out of shape, the flaps hanging from it by partially severed cables.

Minutes later, the Hulk stepped back, breathing hard. His work was finished.

"Dr. Ba . . . eh, ah . . . Hulk."

The man-monster turned slowly from the wreckage and growled, "Urr. Who is bothering Hulk *now?*"

Dr. Irvine stepped hesitantly onto the field from a crew entrance. He blinked nervously at the staring green eyes, devoid of any hint of intelligence and blazing with bestial fury, that watched his every move.

"It's me, Hulk," he said slowly. Irvine held up his shaking hands to show he was unarmed. "I'm your friend, Hulk. Don't you remember?"

The Hulk snarled, his eyes narrowing suspiciously. "Hulk does not know you, little man," he rumbled. "How are you Hulk's friend?"

"Y . . . you must trust me, Hulk," the scientist said, fighting to remain calm in the face of the angry man-monster. "I can help you."

The emerald giant pounded a massive fist against his chest. "Bah! Hulk does not need help from any puny man. Hulk is the strongest one there is!" The big man's brain whirled. All this talk confused the Hulk, made his head hurt.

The raven-haired Miss Winters stepped from the shadows behind Dr. Irvine, tugging her hood away from her face. "Let me try, Doctor," she said softly.

"No," Irvine said quickly. "There's no telling what he might do to you—*and* me right now. I don't think . . ." he started, but the girl brushed quickly past him and stood in front of the Hulk.

The Hulk looked at the girl, his lips curled in an angry snarl.

"Hulk," she said softly.

"Hunh," the green Goliath grunted.

She extended her hand and reached slowly toward the big green man. "Do you remember *me?*" she asked with a smile.

The green giant cocked his head to one side. The girl's face slid momentarily through his mind, partially obscured by a translucent veil of confusion.

"Hulk—remembers," he said at last. "Is girl Hulk's friend?"

"Yes," she nodded, her smile broadening. Miss Winter's fingers brushed lightly against the big green man's tough hide. "I'm Leslie," she told him, "your friend." She laid her hand on his arm.

The Hulk looked at the slim, smooth hand resting on his arm and then at the girl.

"Less-lee," he repeated slowly. His emerald lips

curled suddenly into a smile. "Less-lee. Less-lee is Hulk's friend."

Leslie Winters sighed in relief. The creature's broad smile had startled her. It was not the smile of an evil, deadly monster. It was the smile of a young child delighting in the discovery of something new and wonderful.

"Will you come with me, Hulk?" she asked. "We want to help you."

The man-beast pondered this for a moment before nodding. They were his friends because they had not tried to hurt him like the others did. "Hulk will go with Less-lee," he announced.

The Hulk put out his massive hand. Smiling, Leslie took it and together, they went back into the terminal building. Shaking his head in wonder, Dr. Irvine followed.

Half an hour later, while tense security guards scoured the airport for the Hulk, a Lear jet lifted into the sky from O'Hare's runway 32 Right and disappeared into the falling snow, traveling due east with the thick, storm-swollen clouds.

Chapter 12

"THAT WAS JUST SWELL," TIM COS-
well grumbled. "A day and a half at sea and what do
we get for our troubles? The runaround!"

Peter Parker brushed a lock of brown hair from his
forehead and sighed as the wind blew it back a moment later. *What the heck? Just another of life's little
frustrations to go along with all the others. The navy's
been playing their soggy cards close to their braided
chests since StarLab made the big bye-bye from the
sky yesterday—and if that doesn't frustrate your aver-
age, everyday mild-mannered reporter, I don't know
what will!*

The two reporters slumped moodily down the gang-
plank from the USS *Alexander Hamilton* to the pier in
New Jersey. It was a dark, dingy afternoon with dirty-
looking gray clouds rolling lazily across the sky. A
light, frozen drizzle fell against Peter's face, further
adding to the young photographer's misery.

Tim Coswell was not much happier.

"The government can't do this to us," he complained. "Whatever happened to the first amendment? The people's right to know?" He slapped a hand over his eyes and groaned. "And what's Jameson going to do to me when I come back without a story?"

But something big is up and that's for sure! A naval officer in charge of an atomic-powered aircraft carrier doesn't go into mini-fits for every little thing that goes wrong—unless, of course, his bosses at NASA are hit with the third piece of bad luck in less than two days and he happens to be the guy in charge when it happens.

Peter thoughtfully rubbed his chin. *First I bust in on a computer theft pulled off by a bunch of really well-organized professional hoods and find out they ripped off NASA programming. Then NASA itself is taken for additional software on the next unmanned flight, a job that implies an equally well-organized mob. And now StarLab disappears right out from under their noses—*

—Stolen!

Put them all together and you don't get mother! You get an organization that's beginning to look very big and very powerful!

"He'll fire me for sure," Coswell moaned. "I just know he will. I'll be out of a job—and we've still got twenty-two and a half years to go on the mortgage."

It takes whole oodles of hardware to heist about twenty-five tons of red-hot metal from midair—not to mention the know-how! If they out-technology NASA, they must know something! Yeah, there're some pretty heavy minds and big bucks backing this caper, and last time I looked, people doing good deeds don't go around boosting satellites from Uncle Sam without so much as a "How's your mother, Ed?"

"You've got to help me, Peter," Coswell pleaded. "You've got to tell Jameson that *nobody* could get anything from those navy guys. They just wouldn't talk. You know, you were there. He'll believe you!"

I've got to find those bones I buried. Whatever they're after is up in outer space and that kinda stuff tends to be a bit on the dangerous side!

"You'll do it, won't you, Peter?" Coswell stared ahead into the gloom that hung over the dock. "You'll tell Jameson there was nothing I could do, right?

"Peter?"

Coswell looked around, but Peter Parker was no longer walking beside him. He looked toward the gate and saw the young photographer there, frantically hailing a taxicab cruising by the shipyard.

"Awww, Peter," Coswell moaned miserably as the cab, with Peter Parker inside, sped away from the gate. "What am I going to do about Jameson . . . ?"

Now just why am I finding this so tough to do?
Spider-Man clung to the face of the apartment building across the street from the police station on Manhattan's 80th Street. He crouched like a gigantic spider beneath a protruding air-conditioner sleeve watching the movement of blue uniforms and blue-and-white cars in front of the precinct house.

I've been wanted by the boys in blue so many times for so many things I'm not sure they've had enough time to get all the wanted posters with my picture off the walls. I'd hate myself in the morning if I went sauntering in there and those guys decided the station was the Alamo and I was a Mexican!

Spidey sighed and began crawling down the building. *Well, if I want to get any information on the great NASA rip-offs, inside is where I've got to go, like it or not. I've just got to play it slow and cool.*

The Wall-crawler dropped lightly to the sidewalk, straightened his shoulders and marched with determination to the station house.

He skipped nimbly past an oncoming car and trotted to the opposite side of the street. Several police officers by the precinct door stopped their conversation and watched the Web-slinger approach.

Sheesh! That's all I need to do right now—have one

of those guys slap me with a summons for jaywalking!

"Are you for *real,* buddy?" one of the cops grinned as Spidey came to the door.

"Just here on business, friend," Spider-Man said, keeping his tone light.

The cop lifted his cap and scratched his head. "I mean, are you really Spider-Man or what?"

"Guilty," Spider-Man admitted. *Whoops! Wrong choice of word!*

One of the other officers squinted at the costumed youth. "Ain't Spider-Man still wanted?" he asked the first cop.

"Naw. Not anymore."

"You sure?"

"I haven't seen anything on him lately."

"Excuse me," Spider-Man said as he stepped gingerly past the two officers into the station house. "I'll just go inside while you two argue this out. If you decide you're supposed to bust me, you'll know where I am, right?"

Inside, the police station was a bustle of activity. Cops and plainclothes detectives rushed through doors, up stairs, down stairs, to telephones. In the midst of all this was a lone man, a haven of sanity in the middle of madness, who sat calmly at his desk. The desk sergeant did not look up from his reports when Spider-Man walked up to him.

" 'Scuse me, Sergeant."

Sgt. Dave Orleans said, "Yeah?"

"I was wondering if you could help me," Spidey said.

The man looked up and pursed his lips. "Well, well, well, what have we here?"

"I come in peace," the Web-slinger said. "I need a little help with something I'm working on."

"Oh? Who are you?" Orleans asked calmly.

Spidey looked down the length of his body at the dark-blue-and-red costume. "Sorry I didn't introduce myself, but considering the getup I thought that might be overdoing a bit. I'm Spider-Man."

"Spider-Man."

"Uh-huh. You know, climbing walls, slinging webs, catching crooks. That kind of thing."

"No kidding," Orleans grinned. He took off his glasses. "I should've known that Spider-Man would come waltzing into my station this afternoon. Yesterday it was Captain America, today's Spider-Man, tomorrow's supposed to be Iron Man, and if we're lucky, for Sunday we'll get the whole damned Avengers in!"

"You must be a riot in the locker room, Sarge."

"C'mon, pal. Anyone can put on a funny costume and say he's Spider-Man, though Lord only knows why he'd want to." Sgt. Orleans put on his glasses and turned back to his reports. "Now make like a tree and leave, buster, before I run you in for disturbing my peace," he ordered without looking up.

"Isn't there anything I can say that'll convince you, Sarge?"

Sgt. Orleans flipped through a stack of papers. "Uh-huh. Good-bye would do wonders for your credibility."

"Yeah, but, Sgt. Orleans . . ."

"You're getting on my nerves, kid," the officer snapped and jerked his head up angrily. "I've got . . . a . . . lo . . . ohmigod! You're standing on the ceiling!"

Spider-Man, arms folded across his chest as he stood upside down on the dingy green ceiling, said, "I'll bet that's how come you're a cop, Sarge. You've got the most amazing powers of observation! Now, has my little demonstration convinced you of my identity or do I have to bring in Dillinger before you'll believe me?"

"I believe you," Orleans said. "Believe me, I believe you."

Spidey dropped from the ceiling, somersaulted and landed nimbly on his feet in front of the desk. "No applause please," he said. "I just want to have a few words with the three dudes busted for the computer break-in a couple of nights ago."

Orleans eyed the Web-slinger suspiciously. "What d'you know about that?"

"I busted them for it."

"Oh." The sergeant looked disappointed. "Right. Well, you can't see them."

"Even if I promise not to use the rubber hose on them? Honest, Sarge, all I want to do is ask them a couple of questions."

"You still can't see them."

"Why not?"

"Because they're not here anymore is why. They were charged, booked, arraigned, and bailed out."

"Wonderful."

"They walked out of here about three, four hours ago." Sgt. Orleans leaned forward in his seat. "Say, what the hell's going on, anyway?"

Spider-Man was already walking toward the door. "I don't know. That's what I wanted to ask *them*." He waved over his shoulder. "Thanks for the fun and games, Sarge.

"I'll be in touch."

Chapter 13

NOW WHY THE HELL CAN'T I MOVE, Bruce Banner wondered idly to himself. Somehow, the answer did not seem too important to the young scientist. He knew he was lying on his back on a soft, warm surface, his arms and legs strangely immobile. But he felt warm and secure, well rested as if after a long, refreshing dream.

"Dr. Banner."

The feminine voice floated through his mind. He remembered it from . . . somewhere. A dream?

"I know you can hear me, Dr. Banner. You've been under sedation since yesterday but your bioreadings indicate your system's free of the drug by now."

Then why am I so sleepy?

He suddenly realized he had not answered the voice aloud as he had thought. His eyes snapped open. "Who . . . ?"

Dr. Irvine and Leslie Winters stood watching the young scientist from the other side of a thick pane of glass. He realized he was strapped to a long examination table in a small chamber.

A prisoner!

"He's awake, Dr. Irvine," Miss Winters said, her voice crackling electronically from the speaker on the wall of the chamber.

"What's going on?" Bruce shouted. He strained against the leather straps that held him to the table, but as Bruce Banner, his muscles were inadequate for the task. "What're you doing to me?"

"Calm down, Dr. Banner," Irvine said reassuringly. "We're not going to hurt you."

"But it's all right," Bruce said. "Really. There's no danger of me turning into the Hulk again—not as long as I'm not placed under any strain," he called, trying to sound reasonable. "Please unstrap me."

Dr. Irvine smiled pleasantly. "Ah, but we *want* you to undergo your rather remarkable transformation, my friend. In fact, our plans depend on it."

"Plans?" Bruce sagged onto the table.

Irvine started to speak but stopped when a door opened out of Bruce's line of sight. "Mr. Pendergast, Prof. Warner," he smiled. "You're just in time, gentlemen. Dr. Banner is awake now."

"Excellent, Doctor," the tall, impeccably dressed man said as he stepped in front of the window. Pendergast glanced at the bound man on the table with cold, merciless eyes. "Welcome, Dr. Banner. We've worked for a long time to lure you here."

Bruce Banner studied the slim man with a puzzled expression. "*Lure* me? Where?" He strained once again against the straps as he angrily demanded, "What the hell are you talking about? Why am I being held prisoner?"

"Because we've a great need of your alter ego, Dr. Banner," Pendergast explained evenly. "We planted those stories about the institute discovering a cure for gamma-radiation poisoning in the hope it would draw you to us." Pendergast allowed a cold, humorless smile to cross his solemn face. "Needless to say, Doctor, there is no cure, though even you will have to admit our methods were clever." The smile faded as quickly as it had appeared. "But now we have you and the only thing that interests us is the Hulk."

Bruce was confused. How had he gotten here? What had happened at the airport in Chicago to cause the change? And how had they convinced the bestial Hulk to accompany them to this place—wherever the hell this place was!

"You're insane," Bruce exclaimed. "What possible good can the Hulk do for you? There's no way in the world you could control him."

"On the contrary, my dear colleague," Dr. Irvine chuckled. "The means of controlling your more primitive half is not only within our capability, it's already been implemented."

Dr. Robert Bruce Banner gritted his teeth. He breathed deeply, trying desperately to remain calm. He could feel his face flush as the blood pounded through his veins. I'm being used, he thought bitterly. The awesome power of the Hulk at the command of men engaged in an obviously illegal endeavor frightened the young physicist almost as much as the man-monster himself. I must remain calm, he told himself. I mustn't allow it to happen. As long as I resist the change they can't use the Hulk!

"Come now, Doctor," Irvine crooned sweetly, eyeing his captive's pale, sweating face with satisfaction. "It *is* going to happen, you know. You can't keep the Hulk locked away inside of you forever.

"Not if you wish to leave this cell alive."

Bruce looked into the other man's face. "What . . . ?"

"The walls," Irvine said. He reached over and pressed a button on the wall beside the observation window. Machinery began to hum behind the walls. "They move."

Bruce looked and saw that the walls had indeed begun to move, slowly crawling across the floor toward him. The young scientist's eyes shone with panic and he gulped for breath. God, *no!* his mind screamed. His heart beat like a tom-tom in his thin chest, triggering unknown physical changes within his radiation-mutated body.

And no matter how hard he fought to resist it, Bruce Banner knew it was, as always, inevitable!

Pendergast watched the young scientist writhe on the table with mild interest. Banner's handsome face was contorted, as if he were in great pain.

The walls moved steadily across the floor toward the table.

"Arggghh!"

Dr. Irvine watched in fascination. Prof. Warner stepped before the window, absently fingering his scraggly beard. The young man on the table was changing before their eyes, seeming to grow larger as they watched, his skin taking on a light-green hue. The leather straps around his wrists and ankles creaked as he pulled against them. They snapped easily this time, freeing the young scientist.

He rolled off the table and landed heavily on the floor. He lay there with his whole body trembling. There was no reversing the horrible metamorphosis that gripped him now. His skin grew a darker green, his scrawny muscles thickened and his narrow shoulders broadened. Within seconds, he was struggling to his feet, growling deep in his throat at the approaching walls.

The Hulk was awake.

And he was angry!

"Simply amazing," Prof. Warner whispered in awe. "I never knew the human body was capable of such a remarkable change."

Irvine nodded happily, his eyes wide with delight.

But the green mammoth did not see the men who stood outside his cage studying him with clinical interest. His attention was drawn immediately to the steel walls rumbling toward him from either side. He did not know where he was or how he had gotten here, but that did not matter now. There was danger and that was what was important.

The jade giant charged one wall with a savage roar. His massive green fists rose and then fell against the wall like a wrecking ball. The steel wall buckled under the Hulk's assault. The mechanism that pushed the wall forward ground to a halt.

"Hah!" the man-brute barked. This was one of man's stupider attacks. It was so easy to smash.

The Hulk slapped his hands against the other wall and pushed back at it. But the big green creature's bare feet could not find purchase on the slippery metal floor and he was shoved back until he was slammed into the opposite wall.

He snarled angrily and braced his back against the wall. He swung his feet up to rest against the steel panel that tried to crush him. The Hulk began to straighten his body. The machinery that moved the wall could not long compete with the Hulk's incredible strength, but then, it wasn't really built to. The wall was shoved back, its motors silenced.

"Phenomenal," Prof. Warner exclaimed.

"Yes," Irvine agreed. "But we knew he was powerful, Abraham. The crucial test comes now."

The Hulk turned from the crumpled walls and looked with hate-filled eyes at the men outside the cage. "Huh! You thought walls could kill Hulk!" he bellowed. "But walls of steel could be smashed." He raised a clenched fist before the glass window. "And so can walls of glass!"

Daniel Irvine held a microphone to his mouth. "*No,* Hulk," he said softly. "Put your hand down."

The words buzzed in the green Goliath's ears, words that told him not to crash his way out of this prison, even though he knew he must. He shook his head, but the words were still there and he stopped, lowering his arm.

"Very good, Hulk," he heard in his head. "Now sit down."

The creature dropped to the floor and sat docilely with unblinking eyes.

Pendergast nodded his approval.

"How is this done, Daniel?" Prof. Warner asked.

Dr. Irvine smiled, enjoying the opportunity to show off his accomplishment. "With ultrasonics, Abraham," he said with pride. "You see, I planted a small receiver in Banner's ear which, when activated, emits high-frequency sonic vibrations. These interfere with the Hulk's rather limited thought capacity, thus making him susceptible to my commands, broadcast through the receiver."

"How soon can we begin?" Pendergast asked.

"Anytime now, Mr. Pendergast."

"Fine. The helicopter is waiting outside to transport you and your charge to the target area." Pendergast turned and left the room.

"On your feet, my big green friend," Dr. Irvine ordered into his microphone. "We're taking you on a little journey now. . . ."

The Hulk rose and stood as still as a jade statue in the center of his cell, awaiting orders.

"—into the heart of a live volcano."

Chapter 14

Fun is fun, but swinging around Manhattan tends to lose its appeal after the first three hours!

Spider-Man swung his dark blue-clad legs out before him, propelling himself through the air high above the New York streets. He flew from webbing to webbing, methodically crisscrossing the city. His senses were alert, searching. As soon as he was near those he sought, his spider sense would let him know.

Assuming they're still in the city!

The Web-slinger dropped to a ledge and perched there for a moment searching through the night. *I suppose I shouldn't complain. All things considered, things haven't gone so well for me in a long time. A bunch of two-bit thugs up to no good isn't anything all that new that it should bug me. They're around somewhere and sooner or later our paths are going to cross.*

And when they do, I'm gonna make sure they let me in on their larcenous little secrets! I just hate mysteries!

Once again the Web-slinger launched himself into the night sky. *And even more than that, this particular mystery's keeping me away from one of the more pleasant ways to spend a cold winter eve . . . namely hanging out in front of a nice cozy fireplace in the company of one Ms. Cindy Sayers, lady private eye and all around nifty person.*

The costumed youth chuckled as he swept through the air. *Mr. Parker, you are one lucky arachnid to have a lady like her . . . especially after a couple or three bad-news relationships that were about as successful as George McGovern's 1972 presidential campaign.*

But stability has at last returned to the life of our boy hero and romance is blossoming! Besides that, things couldn't be better on other fronts. Aunt May's in tip-top shape, still worrying about me catching cold, God bless her. Who else would call long distance from her vacation with her cousins in Arizona to remind me to wear my galoshes?

Even Jameson's paying relatively good bucks for my photos and my graduate-school studies have been smooth sailing for the last couple of months!

Sheesh, I hope I can adjust to the sudden shock of all this good luck. I'm just not used to it!

Spidey's deliberate search of Manhattan had brought him back to the southern tip of the island. He swung through the silence of the financial district for several minutes, but his senses alerted him to nothing. The Wall-crawler turned and headed back up north on Broadway.

As usual, Greenwich Village was as alive and busy as ever despite the two feet of snow on the sidewalks and streets, and the arcticlike temperatures that gripped the city. *I don't really think those thugs I'm looking for are going to spend their first night out of the hoosegow sightseeing along Eighth Street, do I?*

Naw, dudes like that'd want to go someplace where they can relax and calm their poor, shattered senses, like a bar!

Spidey turned on to Mercer Street and landed on top of the awning over the entrance to an apartment building. *Seems to me they weren't the type to frequent the bar at the Pierre, so I ought to make a flyby of some of the, ahem . . . sleazier bar districts in the city and see if any of 'em set my senses tinglin'!*

I just hope nobody sees me there. What would my Aunt May say if she heard I went to those kinds of places?

The Wall-crawler fired a strand of webbing at the dark building across the narrow street and took off again. He swiftly swung by the dark, dirty waterfront across town with its dingy bars, but nothing caught his attention there. He headed back uptown along Eighth Avenue.

Between Twenty-ninth and Thirtieth streets his head began to tingle wildly.

Bingo!

Spider-Man grabbed hold of a flagpole jutting from a darkened office building and swung up on it, balancing effortlessly on the slim pole. The intense brown eyes behind the mask searched the streets below.

The door to Al's Tavern on the corner of Thirtieth flew open and three men stumbled out on to the street, laughing drunkenly. They stood swaying in the cold night air for several minutes debating some matter in loud, unintelligible whispers. Spidey's uncanny sixth sense gave the costumed youth another hard twinge as he watched the trio.

I get the message, spidey-sense! Those turkeys are the birds I'm looking for!

Walking unsteadily, the three men lurched to a car parked in the middle of the block. One of them tried several times to find the door lock with a key before another pushed him aside and, laughing hysterically, completed the delicate maneuver. They piled into the car and drove off.

Hooboy! Talking to those cuties is gonna be a real pleasure! I can see it now: I'll be trying to get information from them and they'll be telling me a traveling-salesman joke!

Spidey followed the zigzagging Oldsmobile as it roared through the streets. *Well, try to look on the bright side, m'boy! Maybe they'll be more useful swacked than sober. Maybe they'll get careless and lead me to someone higher up in their organization. . . .*

And maybe sheep will learn to fly.

An hour later, the Web-slinger was beginning to believe his earlier cynicism was not entirely unfounded. *Enough's enough! These bozos have just been meandering in your basic random fashion like a bunch of lost tourists! They're not going to be going anywhere important tonight and I can't afford to wait! So . . .*

The short, dark man named Mandez wiped his thick black mustache with the back of his hand and smacked his lips in satisfaction. "Ah, this hits the spot," he laughed and held up a bottle of cheap whiskey.

Ryan, the muscular blond man behind the wheel of the Oldsmobile, reached for the liquor bottle. "You've hit yer spot enough," he said thickly. "Lemme getta shot o'that."

"Jeez," Mandez said. "I've never been so glad to be outta the slammer in my life! I didn't know we was heisting *government* stuff. I don't wanna get into a *federal* rap." He rubbed his dark face. "Even though Jocko got his hand busted, *he's* the lucky one. *He* got away!"

"Ain't nothin' ya can do about it now, Manny," the man in the backseat said. "Who the hell thought we was gonna run inta Spider-Man? And gimme the bottle awready, fer cryin' out loud!"

Ryan handed the bottle back. "Hell, at least we been bailed out like we was promised and they're gettin' us lawyers."

Mandez hiccuped.

Thwump!

"Whazzat?" Nelson, the man sprawled in the back-seat, sat up quickly, his bloodshot eyes darting about.

Ryan hunched over the wheel. "Dunno," he whispered hoarsely. "Sounded like somethin' landed on the roof!"

"Yeah," Mandez nodded. He peered through the windshield. "I don't see nothing, but I can't tell. Don't take any chances, Ryan. Speed up!"

The driver's foot began to depress the accelerator, sending the speedometer rising slowly.

Kronk!

Ryan yelped in surprise as two scarlet-gloved hands crashed through the roof and slammed into his head.

And to think some people need karate!

The car swerved dangerously into the opposite lane and Spider-Man clung to the roof, staying with it. The street was clear of traffic at the moment and the car was allowed clear access to the brick wall of a building as it jumped the curb.

Spidey jumped off the car's roof at the last instant, somersaulting to safety on the sidewalk. The heavy sedan smashed headlong into the wall, the front end crumbling like cardboard.

The Wall-crawler rushed over to the car. *No sign of fire, good!*

He yanked open the doors. The three thugs were staring at him from inside, shock and surprise on their faces.

"Now what the hell did you do that for?" Mandez asked, blinking.

"I was lonely." Spidey shrugged. "I wanted somebody to talk to. I decided *you* would make the most fascinating conversationalists."

"You hadda smash the *car?*" Ryan said miserably. "Couldn't ya just asked us ta pull over!"

Spidey jerked his thumb over his shoulder. "C'mon, guys," he ordered. "Step into my office where we can talk."

Without warning, Ryan launched himself from the car, wrapping his thick arms around the Web-slinger's waist. His momentum drove Spidey backward and the two men crashed to the ground.

Ryan swung wildly at Spider-Man, but the Web-slinger easily parried the blow and drove his fist into the crook's stomach. Two swift chops to the neck sent the felon sprawling on the ground, out like a light.

Mandez and Nelson, meanwhile, had leaped from the car and were reaching inside their coats for their guns.

"You don't want to do that, fellas," Spider-Man said, rising to one knee.

They drew their pistols.

Spider-Man sprang forward, flinging himself headlong at Nelson. Before the startled thug could readjust his aim, the Wall-crawler was knocking him to the ground. Mandez swung his gun around.

The costumed youth flung himself backward, flipping up on to his hands and kicking his foot out. His booted foot knocked away the automatic. Springing expertly to his feet, Spider-Man grabbed the small man's arm and twisted hard.

"Yeow!" the crook cried, his gun dropping from numb fingers.

"I *told* you you didn't want to do that," Spidey said sharply. "But you *do* want to talk to me, don't you?"

"Hey, I don't have to tal . . . unnhh!" Mandez yelped in pain as Spider-Man yanked sharply on his arm.

"First let me tell you what it is you don't want to talk about, sweetums," the Web-slinger said. "Then you can talk about it anyway!" He gave another sudden pull on the dark man's arm to emphasize his words. "Now then, let's start with who you're working for!"

"I dunno."

"Am I to believe you don't know who hired you?"

"We never saw 'em," Mandez said quickly. "Our orders came over the phone."

"How did you get in touch with them if anything went bad?"

"Hey, listen, man," Mandez protested mildly. "We don't work for no organization or nothing! Some dude hired us over the phone to pull off that one job, that's all! Jocko and me usually work free lance."

"Jocko?"

The little man averted his eyes. He'd said too much.

"Forget it," Spidey said. "He's the one that got away, right? I don't care about him right now. I'm looking for bigger fish!"

"I don't know him. Honest!"

Spider-Man loosened his grip on the other man. "You don't know very much, do you? Problem is, there's a whole boatload of things I *have* to know!"

Mandez saw his chance. "There's someone who might be able to tell you," he offered quickly. "This dude in the Village's up on all kinds of things going down."

Spidey leaned closer to the sweating man. "Who?"

Mandez licked his lips. "Guy they call Sunshine."

"You're kidding."

"I swear it," Mandez said. "Sunshine. He hangs out at the Purple Circle on Christopher Street."

Nodding his head slowly, Spider-Man released Mandez. "Sunshine. Purple Circle. Christopher Street. I'm sorry I *asked*."

Mandez rubbed his aching shoulder. Now maybe that damned costumed creep would go away and leave them alone!

A few minutes later, Spider-Man was leaving, swinging on a strand of his indestructible webbing toward the West Village.

"*Hey!* What about *us?*" Mandez called after him.

Spidey looked over his shoulder at the three men,

their arms webbed securely to their sides, dangling like Christmas ornaments from a lamp post.

"Don't sweat it, creep," he called back happily. "That stuff dissolves sooner or later!"

Chapter 15

THE HUGE JET HELICOPTER STREAKED through the clear, blue skies over the north Pacific Ocean, practically skimming the still waters with its landing gear.

A small island lay dead ahead, a tall, tapering mountain its only noticeable feature. An oil tanker lay anchored half a mile from its shores.

The 'copter whooshed past the tanker's bow and continued toward the island, waiting until the last moment before it gained the necessary altitude to avoid collision with the mountain. Its speed decreased as it reached the peak and began to circle the top.

Dr. Daniel Irvine glanced out the window beside the copilot's seat where he sat. "We're there," he said into the heavy headset he wore. "Is our passenger ready to disembark?" He chuckled into the microphone.

In the cargo hold of the circling chopper, two orange-jump-suited technicians stood on either side of a much larger man clad in a silver protective suit. A square, silver helmet was fastened to his head and a heavy tank was attached to his back. He sat immobile on the floor, his emerald-green eyes staring blankly through the narrow view plate.

"The Hulk is ready, sir," one of the technicians said into his mike.

"Did you hear that, Argosy?" Irvine asked.

"We read you, Transport One," a voice crackled back from the tanker. "We are standing by."

"All right," the scientist said to the pilot. "Take it down!"

The helicopter dropped sharply and flew over the top of the mountain where it was throttled back into a hover. The peak was not a plateau; rather there was nothing atop the high mountain. Nothing but a gaping, black hole. The pilot deftly maneuvered the chopper over to the mouth of the hole, mere feet from the rocky wall.

"You may stand now, Hulk," Dr. Irvine ordered gently into the mike.

The seven-foot-tall emerald giant rose obediently to his feet. One of the technicians stepped to the huge sliding doors at the side of the hold and pulled them open.

"To the door, my brutish friend."

The Hulk stepped to the door, obeying the words that buzzed like an annoying insect in his ear.

"And out you go!"

Without hesitation, the man-brute calmly stepped from the hovering helicopter.

He landed with a thud on the steep wall of the volcano, his heavy body sending a shower of small stones clattering into the dark hole. Even after long moments, they could not be heard hitting bottom.

"I want you to climb *down* into the hole, Hulk," the doctor said softly. "It will be very hot, but between the suit you wear and your supertough skin, you should be adequately protected."

Almost mechanically, the jade Goliath began a slow, deliberate climb into the yawning pit, his hands and feet smashing out finger and toe holes as he went along.

"You are to descend until you reach the huge machine that lies down there."

Mindlessly, the man-brute grunted, continuing his descent. But soon, he grew weary of the tedious hand-over-hand repetition into the pitch blackness. He pushed himself from the wall and allowed himself to drop into the bottomless pit!

The air grew hotter and hotter as the Hulk fell, heating the silver surface of his protective suit. Instinctively, the green mammoth angled his massive body, controlling his headlong plunge into the abyss.

He fell for long minutes until, at last, a red glow became visible far below. It grew larger as he came closer, until it became apparent the red glow was from the fires at the very heart of the volcano! The air around the descending man-creature was unbreathable, enough to sear even the lungs of the mighty Hulk were it not for the built-in oxygen supply he wore on his back.

The Hulk manuevered himself, drawing closer to the red-hot wall of the volcano. His fingers touched the wall, then began to sink into the rock, deeper and deeper as he applied pressure. His massive fingers gouged five deep grooves in the rock as he dug in, slowing his plunge.

He came to a stop several yards above the sloping floor at the bottom of the miles-deep pit. Even through the thick protective suit, the Hulk could feel the great heat against his emerald skin, but he paid it no mind. Directly below his dangling feet was a river of molten lava that flowed between the two shores of red-hot, glowing rock. The walls around him shimmered with the red-and-blue heat from the Earth's bowels.

He dropped to the near-molten rock.

Mindlessly he shuffled forward, his insulated booted feet sloshing through liquid rock. The air burned around him, making it difficult to see, but still he shambled on—following orders.

He followed the downward-slanting tunnel along its course, smashing aside burning, red obstructions, wading through pools of molten ore that mostly covered his boots but sometimes came up to his waist.

Several minutes later he came to a massive pile of glowing crimson rocks that blocked his path. He did not hesitate. Slogging through the sucking lava, he charged the obstruction.

The rocks seemed to explode as the Hulk bored through them like a human wrecking ball. He skidded awkwardly to a halt on the other side, swinging his large arms to keep his balance.

And there, before the panting, sweating man-monster sat the glowing, red-hot remains of StarLab I!

A sensor beeped sharply on the console before Dr. Irvine in the cockpit of the circling helicopter. The sensor was connected to one strapped to the Hulk's chest, tuned to certain insulated instruments aboard StarLab.

The beast had done it!

"Excellent, Hulk," he cooed happily into the mike. "Now I want you to pick up the big machine." He smiled. "Bring it out of the volcano to the boat waiting for you."

The Hulk's hands sank into the molten skin of the huge satellite. Almost twenty tons of half-melted machinery was lifted from the ground and shifted slowly onto the creature's broad back. He staggered under the enormous weight, shifting the red-hot space vehicle until it was comfortably balanced.

Slowly, the Hulk started back the way he had come. His recent passage through the tunnel near the Earth's core had left it clear of obstacles so, despite his burden, the green Goliath reached his starting point in less time than it had taken to find StarLab.

He gingerly placed the satellite on the bubbling ground. Going back up the way he had come was impossible. Two miles of sheer walls awaited him that way and, though he could make it unhindered, Star-Lab would have to remain behind.

His dull eyes passed over the walls of the tunnel. Steaming lava seeped from small cracks at one point, streaming into a narrow river that flowed into the passage. He drew back his gloved fist and, grunting, sent it smashing through the rock.

The red-hot substance cracked easily and more lava bubbled from the new holes. Several more blows opened a crack as tall as the man-brute and twice as wide. Suddenly, a red-hot wave of lava splashed through and broke over the Hulk. He staggered backward and tumbled quickly out of the way.

The flood of molten rock abated after several seconds, only to be replaced by a stream of bubbling hot water that turned instantly to billowing clouds of steam on contact with the rock.

The Hulk wiped the steam from his view plate with a swipe of his massive paw. The lava and water had widened the hole he had started so that it was now large enough for both the green giant and StarLab to pass through.

And, if the water was any indication, this new passage led straight out into the sea.

The insulation in his protective suit was beginning to smolder by the time the jade-hued giant replaced the forty thousand pounds of seemingly ruined spaceship on his back. He stepped into the flowing stream and waded slowly through the bubbling, boiling water.

The tunnel slanted upward almost immediately, sloping gradually enough for the big green man to keep his footing. His feet sank deep into the soggy dust floor making walking even more difficult.

"Come to me, Hulk," buzzed in his ear. "Bring me

the prize from the center of the Earth!" the voice urged softly.

The man-monster plodded steadily on with his burden, climbing back up toward the light of day from the Stygian darkness of the volcano.

The water level began to rise as the wide passage leveled after over two miles. Then, suddenly, a heavy stone wall marked the end of the tunnel.

A pool of water rippled before the natural barricade, seeping into a channel eroded into the rock by ages of flowing water. The Hulk bent his thick body forward and dumped the charred remains of StarLab into the pool. The still-red-hot metal sizzled loudly as it sank into the clear, deep water, sending up plumes of steam that swirled through the cavern. The silver-suited colossus dove in after it.

The man-monster swam straight down the underwater tunnel, one great hand pushing the satellite before him. A hundred yards down, the passage gave way to the open sea.

"To the boat, Hulk," the soothing voice commanded.

The green-skinned behemoth kicked his powerfully muscled legs and headed to the surface with one hand dragging the twisted wreckage behind him. Seconds later, his head poked out of the sea into the air, a quarter of a mile from the waiting tanker.

The pilot of the hovering chopper spotted the burst of sunlight flashing off the man-brute's protective headgear and pointed it out to Dr. Irvine. The scientist smiled, picked up a pair of binoculars, and focused them on the bobbing figure below. He saw the image of the blackened hull of the space laboratory undulating beneath the waves.

"I am proud of you, my hulkish helper," he beamed. "All that remains to be done is to take your cargo to the boat and then we may *all* go home!"

Chapter 16

"Now *that* IS KINKY," THE CURLY-blond-haired man nodded approvingly as the front door to the Purple Circle opened and the muscular youth in a dark-blue-and-red costume walked in.

"Glad you like it, chuckles," Spider-Man mumbled as he glanced around the private club on Greenwich Village's Christopher Street. His face twisted into a grimace of distaste beneath his thick mask. The single large room was painted black with dayglow patches of dark purple scattered about the walls and ceiling. A long bar ran along the wall adjacent to the door. The rest of the floor space was taken up by small circular tables clustered around a ten-foot-square dance floor. Light was supplied by black light bulbs that seemed to give the dingy bar an eerie, phosphorescent glow.

Several colorfully dressed men sat at the bar alone or in pairs and four tables were occupied. A Judy Garland song blared from the jukebox.

"Can I help you, friend?" the blond man asked pleasantly.

"I'm looking for somebody," Spidey said, his eyes roaming over the dozen or so occupants in the club for a clue to the man named Sunshine.

The man sighed. "Aren't we all?" he said wistfully. "Are you a member of the PeeCee?" His eyes traveled doubtfully up and down the Web-slinger's colorfully garbed figure.

"Heavens no," Spidey answered. "I'm looking for a guy named, er . . . Sunshine. Know 'im?"

The man frowned at Spider-Man. "Maybe."

"Look, I'm . . ."

"Really," the man said. "I read the *Daily Bugle*. I know who you are."

"Some people tell me Sunshine hangs out here. Is he here or not?"

The blond man chewed thoughtfully at the inside of his cheek, rubbing a slender hand across his forehead. "Well, I suppose you're all right," he said at last. He indicated a table at the very rear of the room, one situated in shadows. For the first time, Spidey noticed a man seated in the shadows.

"Thanks." He nodded to the blond man and walked toward the back.

"*Un*cool, Spider-Man," Sunshine tsked as the Web-slinger stepped up to his table. "I mean, walking up to me after *announcing* your presence to the *whole* world! Don't you have *any* subtlety whatso*ever?*"

"Sorry, Sunshine. I don't have the luxury of subtlety," Spidey said, pulling a chair over from another table and sitting with his arms folded across its back. "Mainly 'cause I ain't got time!"

The slender dark-haired man with a neat, closely trimmed beard leaned forward in his chair. His chocolate-brown face was shiny with perspiration, his black eyes squinting at the Wall-crawler. Spidey could see he was wearing a white silk shirt that seemed to glow in the black light. He also wore a single gold stud in his right earlobe.

"*Every*body's got time, brother," Sunshine said. He lifted a glass of amber liquid to his lips and sipped it slowly to prove his point.

"Not the folks who ripped off StarLab. I'm betting they're planning something for real soon now."

Sunshine stopped with his glass halfway to his mouth. "Who *said* it's been ripped off, Spider-Friend? *I* haven't heard any such news flash on *my* little transistor radio."

Spidey's head tingled slightly. *Ah-ah! I seem to be getting close to something here. Momma's little boy Sunshine is sure as shootin' nervous about something I just said; except he doesn't plan on telling.*

Unless I appeal to his better instincts!

"Something's been going on for a couple of days now, Sunshine. NASA's been hit by two, count 'em, two robberies in as many days involving flight information and programming on their next unmanned mission. Then anywhere from twenty-five to fifty tons of plummeting NASA hardware is suddenly *not* recovered by the navy after disappearing from their radar. I want to know what all those separate numbers add up to!"

Sunshine shrugged elaborately. "Well, I'm *sorry,* Spider-Person, but I . . ."

Spider-Man leaned closer to the table. "I get nervous when big things are happening and nobody fills me in on them, friend," he said softly, menacingly. "And a little birdie tells me you're one of the nobodies not filling me in on this."

The slender black man tried to stare the costumed youth down, but the eerie, white orbs of his mask made him nervous. He averted his eyes. "I've got to cop the *Fifth,*" he whispered through clenched teeth. "I mean, *okay,* there *is* something up, but there're some big, *powerful* people messed up in it. People who can get me *hurt!*"

"I hate to resort to a cliché, Sunny, but I can do some hurting myself if necessary."

"No," Sunshine said quickly. "It *won't* be necessary.

Listen, Spider-Man, my stock in trade is *words,* information. I don't like to *soil* myself with the *seamier* aspects of this business. Okay, some real heavies *have* got something going, but *all* I can tell you is to look outside of Niagara Falls, along the river."

Spider-Man stood. "That's a lot more than I knew before, Sunshine," he nodded. "Thanks."

The black man looked up. "For what? I never said a *thing.*"

Chapter 17

THE SUN SHONE BRIGHT IN THE cloudless sky over the city of Niagara Falls, New York. The evening before, the temperature had begun to rise, reaching, by late this morning, the upper forties. The two feet of hard, icy snow was melting slowly into piles of soggy slush. Even the frozen-over Niagara River was thawing under the bright sun. Trickles of water flowed silently downriver toward the now-silent, stilled falls.

Lovely country, Spider-Man mused. *Too bad I'm not here to admire the scenery.*

The Web-slinger clung upside down to a branch from a tree that stood within four feet of the high chain-link fence surrounding the private industrial complex several yards off the shore of the Niagara River.

A truck hauling a flatbed trailer was roaring up the road to the fence's one gate, black diesel smoke puffing from its exhaust pipe. The truck's bulky cargo was hidden from view beneath a tarpaulin.

A piercing tingle flashed through the Wall-crawler's head.

My goodness gracious, what have we here that makes the old spidey-sense go buzz-buzz?

A pair of guards dressed in gray uniforms stood inside the compound behind the gate, their hands resting easily on the pistols at their sides. They looked carefully at the identification presented by the truck's driver and conferred with the man for several seconds through the fence before electronically opening the gates to allow the truck through.

Now you aren't gonna let that big, bad, mysterious truck just vanish off into the sunset, are you, Mr. Parker?

Nope!

Spider-Man pulled himself upright and perched on the tree limb to survey the setup. Ten feet beyond the fence stood a squat concrete bunker, several feet lower than the top of the fence. Five more bunkers ringed the perimeter of the enclosed compound, all facing the much larger, four-story structure set at the far end of the area. Behind the hangarlike concrete building, the Niagara River wound its way to the famed falls.

The smoke-belching truck rolled slowly through the compound toward the large, windowless hangar.

Signs dotted the fence at regular intervals: DANGER. ELECTRICAL FENCE. 10,000 VOLTS. INSTITUTE FOR RADIATION RESEARCH.

Well, dis mus' be da plaze 'cause dere ain't no udder plaze dat looks like dis plaze! There's nothing else along the river that fits in with what Sunshine told me, and my spidey-sense going off as soon as that truck came along cinches it for this little Web-head! The Institute for Radiation Research definitely ain't what it'd want people to think it is—whatever that is!

The armed guards were two dozen feet to the Wall-crawler's left. They were talking, their attention directed away from Spidey's portion of the fence.

That fence is real hot stuff. If I don't do this trick just right, I'm liable to wind up one overdone little superhero!

Spider-Man stood on the branch, bouncing up and down gently on the tips of his toes. Then he jumped up and landed on the tree limb which gave under his weight, and then sprang back up, propelling the Web-slinger through the air. He arched over the fence in a curled position and straightened as he neared the bunker. Flipping over in a somersault and landing on the edge of the bunker's roof, he quickly dropped flat against the surface.

Spidey peered cautiously over the edge. *All's quiet on the western front, which I take to mean as nobody spotting my rather sensational entrance. And here I was hoping to be discovered by the coach for the Olympic gymnastic team!*

He crawled to the other side of the roof and looked down the gap between the bunker he was on and the next one over. It was deserted.

In fact, the entire compound seemed deserted.

Either everybody's out to lunch at McDonald's right now or I managed to get here in time for some kind of big event!

As he approached the larger building at the end of the compound Spider-Man could make out the sound of the diesel engine coming from around back. He ran in a crouch to the nearest wall and leaped up on it, climbing as fast as he could to the top. He pulled himself up on the roof and ran along the edge to the rear of the hangar.

Now that looks like it could be interesting!

Hidden from view of the main gate and the road that passed a hundred feet from it, at the rear of the building was a pair of hangar doors, now standing open to admit the cumbersome truck and trailer.

Those doors are big enough for a jumbo jet to fit

*through. So why is it I doubt they use this place as a
747 parking garage?*

A dozen men in orange jump suits watched the
truck back into the hangar. While their attention was
on that, Spidey dropped quickly on a strand of webbing to the top of the doorway and swung inside. He
scurried swiftly to the steel-beamed ceiling.

The Web-slinger secreted himself behind a beam
and looked down forty feet to check out the interior
of the hangar.

Below him stretched a vast concrete floor. In the
center of the massive room was what appeared to be
a steel cover, some thirty feet wide. Several men in
laboratory smocks stood on the metal plate with a man
in an expensive suit, watching silently as the truck
squealed to a stop before them.

*And the prize, for best guess without a single clue
to go on, goes to the wonderful, all-purpose spidey-
sense! Don't leave home without that, Karl Malden!*

Several technicians rushed over to the truck from
the sidelines and began to peel back the tarpaulin.
Within moments, the charred, half-melted remains of
StarLab I lay exposed on the long flatbed.

*Well, it may not look like much anymore, but
there's obviously something of great value left in all
that wreckage for those dudes to want it bad enough
to swipe it like they did.*

"Well, Prof. Warner? Are you satisfied?" The well-
dressed man's voice echoed up through the huge, high-
ceilinged hangar so that Spider-Man could hear him
as well as if he stood next to the speaker forty feet below.

"Oh, yes. It's in far better shape than I'd anticipated, Mr. Pendergast," one of the men in a smock
said. "And thank God my calculations were correct.
The main crew compartment, being the most vulner-
able spot on the ship because of its human cargo,
would be the most heavily shielded and insulated
against great heat, impact, et cetera, thus enabling it

to survive the heat of reentry even though better than
a quarter of it was totally incinerated."

The second man in white said, "I'm still amazed
you were able to snatch it out of orbit."

"Well, Daniel," the man called Warner said, "it
really wasn't all that difficult. We could have overrid-
den NASA's control of the vehicle's systems with our
computers, but that would've been practically worth-
less since StarLab's own engines were inadequate to
save the ship. So, we launched a series of drone rockets which rendezvoused with the ship while it was still
in orbit, attached themselves to it and flew StarLab
from the navy's target area.

"Not only that," Warner said, "the drones set up
an electronic field to interfere with their radar to make
it appear as if StarLab had suddenly just vanished."

"How much time will you need to get things ready,
Professor?" Pendergast asked.

Warner toyed thoughtfully with his scraggly white
beard as he regarded the partially melted space station
being lifted from the truck with a crane. "Two days,"
he said. "I've got to strip the on-board computer of all
its programming and components and then refit them
into our satellite and navigation system."

Pendergast consulted his watch. "It is now noon.
Can you have the completed package on the pad and
ready for the final countdown at two o'clock the day
after tomorrow?"

"I said two days, Mr. Pendergast. Yes."

*Satellite? Completed package? Pad? Final count-
down?*

Confused by what he had just heard, Spider-Man
took a closer look at the hangar. For the first time, he
noticed hydraulic pumps on either side of the ceiling;
there, he reasoned from their location and looks, to
swing open the ceiling. A narrow crack ran down the
center of the steel cover in the floor, as if that was
where it separated when the cover was rolled back.

Hydraulics to open the roof.

Some kind of pit in the middle of the floor.

*Now, I know space shots are supposed to take place
in Florida with a lot of palm trees waving all over the
place and Walter Cronkite supplying the running commentary, but something tells me nobody ever told
these guys that's how it's done!*

Pendergast nodded curtly to the two scientists and
left, his heels clicking loudly against the concrete floor.

"Between you and me, Abraham," Dr. Irvine said
when the tall man was out of earshot, "do you think
it's going to work?"

"Why not?" The bearded scientist shrugged. "With
the equipment we can cannibalize from StarLab, our
satellite will have one of the finest guidance and navi-
gational systems currently in use."

Irvine waved his hand impatiently through the air.
"I know the rocket and satellite are going to function,
Abraham. What I'm worried about is the microwave
transceiver."

Warner stiffened indignantly.

"I'm well aware that you created, designed, and
built it, old friend. After all, who put you in contact
with Pendergast and his combine and helped convince
them to back the project?"

"I appreciate that, Daniel. You know that."

"I don't want gratitude, Abraham. I just want to be
sure your satellite will do what it's supposed to. There's
too much at stake here to risk . . ."

"I am sure," Warner said coolly, "my microwave
transceiver will perform exactly as it was designed to:
it will link our satellite with the output circuits of every
communications, weather, and intelligence satellite in
orbit around the planet and transmit every bit of data
that passes through them back to us."

*I think this is the part where I'm supposed to whis-
tle in surprise and say "So that's what these dastardly
fiends are up to!"*

"Calm down, Abraham," Daniel Irvine said. "You
know I have complete faith in your abilities. I'm just
nervous, I guess. Prelaunch jitters or some such." He
shoved his hands into the pockets of his smock. "No,

damn it, I'm nervous because everything's gone so well up till now. I mean, considering the risks we took breaking into that computer office in New York and NASA in Houston, as well as getting StarLab, we've been extraordinarily lucky. I just can't help feeling that our good luck can't last much longer."

And that's all I need to hear from these bozos!

"You're so right, Doc!" Spider-Man slid rapidly to the floor on a strand of webbing. " 'Cause your friendly neighborhood Spider-Man is here to tell you that as of this very instant, your luck has been officially recalled by the factory. And wouldn't you know it? The warranty's *expired!*"

"Spider-Man!" Dr. Irvine gasped.

"You've got a way with words, Doc, I'll give you that much," Spidey said. "Maybe you can use that skill to get yourself a new job once I close this place down. Don't you guys know shooting a big firecracker into space is illegal?"

Prof. Warner backed away from the Web-slinger, his face turning as white as his full beard. "Gu . . . guards!" he called weakly.

"That's not nice, friend," Spidey sighed.

"And totally unnecessary as well, Abraham," Dr. Irvine added, recovering from the surprise of Spider-Man's sudden appearance.

"Why? You planning on beating me to death with all your diplomas, Doc?"

Irvine reached into the pocket of his smock. "No, my fine webbed friend," he spat. "But I *do* have someone at my disposal who is perfectly capable of taking care of you without my help!" He whipped out a small box, about the size of a transistor radio, and brought it to his mouth. "Come to me, my brutish slave," he called into it. "I need you *now!*" . .

"If that's supposed to scare me, fella, forget it. I've had more mad-scientist types threaten me with more of their little toy terribles than you could shake a stick at and, as you can see, I'm still around to tell you that it just *don't* work."

"Ah, Spider-Man," Irvine grinned. "Whereas that may have been true with others, I can assure you that *my* monster is no toy!"

Crrash!

As if those words were a cue, the wall behind Spider-Man seemed to explode into chunks of flying concrete and dust. A ten-foot-square section of the reinforced cement wall that served to partition off the huge room was suddenly no longer there.

Spidey whirled.

Seven feet of jade-hued man-creature stood by the ruined wall, his massive chest rising and falling with each angry breath.

"*My* monster," Dr. Irvine chuckled proudly, "is the Hulk!"

Hoo-boy! So why is it I suddenly feel like a kid named David? At least he had a slingshot to use against his Goliath!

Chapter 18

THE HULK GROWLED IN ANGER AS HE ambled through the gaping hole in the wall. The man-monster's emerald-green eyes blazed with hate beneath the primitive, protruding brow, fixing Spider-Man with a glare the Web-slinger could not remember seeing in the eyes of a civilized man.

Only wild beasts!

Spider-Man held up his hands before him and backed slowly away.

"Hulk . . . hurt little . . . man," the man-brute snarled hesitantly.

"Whoa there, big fella," the Web-slinger said carefully. "Let's not start something that one of us won't be able to finish!"

Namely me!

Dr. Irvine chuckled. "I wouldn't advise you to try reasoning with my jade friend, Spider-Man," he said. "You haven't the time.

"*Kill* Spider-Man!" he commanded into the small box.

The Hulk charged the Web-slinger, his thickly muscled arms reaching for Spidey. The Wall-crawler held his ground until the man-monster was almost upon him and then leaped straight up, flipping effortlessly over the Hulk's head and landing on his feet behind the big green man. The Hulk roared in rage and spun around faster than the Web-slinger had anticipated, his balled fist grazing the costumed youth's chin.

Spider-Man flew backward as if hit by a sledgehammer.

Oh, momma!

He thudded against a wall and crumpled to the floor in pain. *Whew.* Spider-Man shook his head and watched as the twin images of the Hulk merged into one and the loud ringing in his ears subsided. *Maybe if I look upon this is as an educational experience it won't hurt as much!* The Web-slinger braced his back against the wall and slowly started to rise. *Offf! And then again, maybe not!*

His bestial face contorted in rage, the mighty Hulk lumbered toward his foe. He aimed another powerful blow at Spider-Man's head.

Spidey ducked under the massive fist. It shot, unchecked, over his lowered head and smashed through the heavy concrete wall behind him.

Now here's a definite case of a boy who doesn't know his own strength!

As the Hulk reached down to grab his shoulders, Spider-Man threw himself forward and rolled quickly through the man-brute's spread legs.

But since I do, I'd better make it my business to stay away from those sledgehammers he calls fists! Anybody who can break through a concrete wall like it was so much tissue paper can do more damage to my poor little body than I care to think about!

Before the Hulk could turn to continue his attack, Spider-Man swung his legs up and rammed them as hard as he could into the small of the creature's broad back. The green Goliath grunted and stumbled forward.

So what if Kidney punches aren't very nice? Neither is having seven feet worth of really ticked-off green monster sicced on you!

But the Web-slinger's blow only served to increase the Hulk's already prodigious anger. The green mammoth spun, bellowing his surprise and pain as he threw his body at Spidey.

Spider-Man sidestepped the charging man-brute and grabbed hold of one of his thick arms between his gloved hands. The creature's momentum gave the Wall-crawler just the leverage he needed to begin spinning around like a child's top, whirling the Hulk about faster and faster.

"Let go of Hulk!" the big green man roared.

"Sure thing, tall, green, and ugly."

Spider-Man suddenly released his hold on the Hulk's arm and the man-monster took off like a shot, flying uncontrollably through the air.

Kersmash!

The Hulk streaked like a great green missile into the side of the parked flatbed trailer, now empty of its cargo. The impact totaled the vehicle and wrapped the wreckage around the stunned colossus like a straitjacket.

And if that don't take care of that, I don't know what will!

Growling deep in his throat, the Hulk flexed his mighty muscles and split the restraining metal in two.

. . . I don't think I know what will. . . .

"Now stupid bug-man is in big trouble," the Hulk snarled. "Nobody hurts Hulk and gets away with it! Not army, not humans, and not puny little bug-eyed man!"

"You wanna know something, Greenie? I think you really mean it!"

A single, effortless leap brought the Hulk to Spider-Man's side. A jade-hued fist wrapped itself into the

youth's costume and the Hulk yanked Spider-Man
roughly from the floor.

"Yikes!"

"You," the Hulk growled. "You make fun of Hulk,
huh?" The big green man shook the dangling Web-
slinger like a rag doll. "Well, Hulk is sick and tired of
listening to your big mouth, bug-eyes! Even if voice
did not tell Hulk to smash you, Hulk would do it anyway!"

Voice?

"You know something else, handsome?" the costumed youth said. "You're about three times as stupid
as I've been led to believe!" With that, Spider-Man
brought one hand up to the Hulk's face and pressed
the button concealed beneath his glove. A thick stream
of sticky web fluid squirted into the green giant's face.

"Arrgghh!"

The Hulk dropped Spidey to the floor and began
tearing at the webbing with his hands. The thick, viscous chemical blinded him and was beginning to
smother him.

The webbing came away from his face in thick
gobs.

*Uh-oh. That's not supposed to give way that easily
—which leads me to suspect there's plenty of truth to
that old saying by Confucious: Never underestimate
the power of large, green persons more than two or
three times if you still want to be around for dinner!*

The last of the webbing pulled free and the Hulk
snarled cruelly. "So bug-eyes is still here, huh? Bug-
eyes *wants* to be smashed by Hulk!"

"Truth to tell, Hulkie baby, I *could* live without
that. In fact, that's probably the only way I *will* live."

The Hulk charged in swinging. Spider-Man had to
avoid those fists at all costs! One punch was enough to
kill him. His incredible reflexes allowed the Wall-
crawler to dodge, duck, and weave around the Hulk's
fists, staying just ahead of the lethal blows.

Can't keep this up forever. I'm already getting

*winded while Tiny looks fresh as a daisy and ready to
go fifteen rounds with King Kong!*

Spider-Man threw himself to the floor, rolled, and
came up under the Hulk's fists. *So it's time for May
Parker's nephew Peter to put on a few of the old de-
fensive moves—*

The Web-slinger butted his head into the green behemoth's heavily muscled stomach with a force that
would have sent a dozen men reeling. The big green
man merely grunted in discomfort and bent at the
waist, but still, to Spidey's amazement, stayed on his
feet.

*—and then shift quickly to the offense . . . and I do
mean quick!*

He fired a strand of webbing at the steel-beamed
ceiling and, as agile as the creature from which he took
his name, Spider-Man scurried up the thin line. The
Hulk straightened, roaring in anger and frustration.

The man-monster swiped at the climbing Web-
slinger's legs. Spidey swung his legs up and, on the
backswing, slammed his heels into the back of the
Hulk's head.

"Come down now, stupid bug-eyes," the Hulk bellowed, shaking his fist at Spidey. "Bah! You cannot
get away from the Hulk up there, bug! Anywhere you
go, Hulk can go too!"

The Hulk crouched and shot up into the air. The
giant green missile flashed toward Spider-Man, twenty
feet over the floor.

"Don't you *ever* give up, handsome?" Spider-Man
clutched tightly to his webbing with one hand. *Only
have one shot at this so I'd better not blow it, 'cause if
I do, it'll only take one punch from him to make sure
there won't be enough of me left to hit the ground!*

Before the green-skinned behemoth reached him,
Spider-Man released his hold on the webbing. He
curled into a ball and rolled through the air. He
landed on the Hulk's back.

Spidey wrapped his legs around the Hulk's stomach
and his arms around his throat. Plummeting as he was

to the floor twenty feet below, the Hulk ignored the nuisance on his back for the moment. But as soon as his broad feet slammed onto the concrete floor, he reached behind his back, snarling.

"Ha! Bug-eyes is even stupider than army! At least when Hulk smashes machines, they *stay* smashed!"

"Yeah, well, we can't all be Rhodes scholars like you, Hulkie," Spidey said through clenched teeth. He was pulling as hard as he could against the man-monster's neck, trying to choke the big green man into unconsciousness. But the Hulk had only to tighten his uncannily powerful throat muscles to make that move useless.

Wouldn't you know it? This bozo's got a tree stump for a neck!

The Hulk's hands closed around Spidey's upper arms and pulled him effortlessly from the man-monster's back. He dashed the man to the ground.

"Oooff!" Spider-Man felt the breath explode from his lungs. He gasped, trying to suck air into his chest, but the Hulk placed one large foot on his chest, pressing the Wall-crawler to the floor.

"You bother Hulk. You talk to Hulk like Hulk is stupid and does not know what you are saying! You think Hulk does not know you make fun of Hulk!"

"Would it help if I said I was sorry?" Spidey gasped. The foot pressed down harder.

"No more talk, bug-eyes!" the Hulk roared. "Now voice says Hulk must *squash* stupid bug!"

Spider-Man did not stop to ponder the mysterious "voice" the Hulk spoke of. Not while the superhumanly powerful jade giant was slowly increasing the pressure on his chest. He could not breathe.

Gasping, the Wall-crawler grabbed the big, emerald foot planted on his chest. It would not budge.

The Web-slinger groaned in pain. *His oth—other foot . . . yeah!*

With his last remaining bit of strength, Spider-Man lashed out his arm and landed a resounding blow on the green behemoth's kneecap. The Hulk's leg buckled slightly and the pressure on Spidey's chest eased momentarily while the man-brute shifted his weight to regain his balance.

In that instant, Spidey heaved the foot up and the man-monster toppled.

Gasp! The proverbial closeness that too much of isn't comfortable!

Shaking his head and blinking away the black spots that floated before his eyes, Spider-Man rose unsteadily to his feet.

The Hulk was already up and waiting.

"Oh fer cryin' out loud!" Spider-Man groaned.

The jade-hued giant easily grabbed the weakened Wall-crawler and he squeezed the smaller man to his chest.

"Hah!" the green behemoth barked. "Where is all of bug-eye's big talk now?"

The Hulk squeezed the costumed youth tighter to his thick chest, determined to complete the task that he had begun moments before by squashing this bothersome insect. Pains that had not yet begun to fade flared into fresh, blazing agony in the Web-slinger's chest and ribs.

Striking in desperation, Spider-Man clapped his hands over the Hulk's ears. A tiny round object popped out and bounced to the floor.

Immediately, the look of rage vanished from the green giant's face and was replaced by a frown of bewilderment. He looked at the dark-blue-and-red-costumed man clutched to his chest and screwed his brow into folds of concentration, as if trying to determine who this was and what he was doing here.

"Huh?" he rumbled slowly. "What kind of trick is this, bug-man?"

The Hulk released the Web-slinger who folded limply to the cold, hard floor. *Gasp! So that was the voice he was talking about! That was some kind of receiver planted in his ear with those second-rate Wernher Von Brauns on the transmitting end!*

Half a dozen men in orange jump suits ran into

the room from a partitioned-off section of the huge hangar. The dark-haired man in the lead was carrying a bulky rifle with a small canister attached to the stock. Dr. Irvine, remaining behind the line of men, shouted angry orders to the technicians.

"Hurry! Spider-Man's dislodged the control device from the Hulk's ear! There's no telling who he'll turn on now!"

Spider-Man struggled to his knees.

Unh! Even my pain hurts. Feels like about the only thing my ribs would be good for now is barbecuing!

And even though I never considered myself to be particularly masochistic, I've got to attract the Hulk's attention again and convince him I'm really on his side.

"Hulk!"

The emerald colossus had shambled to the demolished flatbed and was studying it carefully. He turned slowly at the Wall-crawler's call, his confusion turning once more to anger as he saw the six technicians running at him with a weapon.

At last he had something to fight that he could understand, even if he did not fully understand why he was fighting.

"The gas, damn it!" Irvine screamed. "Use it before he gets his hands on you!"

The armed man skidded to a stop not a dozen feet from the groggy Web-slinger and took aim at the Hulk as he loped toward them with bared teeth and clenched fists.

Fsssssst!

A cloud of gray gas bubbled from the nozzle of the man's weapon and expanded rapidly to surround first Spider-Man and then the rampaging Hulk. The Wall-crawler tried to hold his breath, but the sharp stab of agony that shot through his side when he tried made him gasp in pain, and inhale the foul-smelling fumes. Almost instantly, he felt himself go numb all over.

It took the Hulk longer to succumb to the grayish cloud—but not much. Before he had covered half the distance to the six brightly garbed men, he collapsed with a sorrowful cry of anger beside Spider-Man.

The technicians waited until the gas had dispersed before walking, followed by Dr. Irvine, to their unconscious captives.

"Now, how . . . ?" the scientist murmured.

Mr. Pendergast, his secretary at his heels, rushed through the door to the center of the hangar.

"Just what in the hell is going on here, Dr. Irvine?" he demanded angrily, his cold gray eyes flashing.

Irvine shrugged. "I—I don't know, Mr. Pendergast," he said with a shake of his head. "Somehow Spider-Man found out about us and . . ."

"Yes," Pendergast nodded, his mouth a cold, cruel line. "I was afraid something like this might happen when he interfered with the New York robbery." He sighed in resignation. "But it would appear that the worst has already happened and we are still in operation despite it. So I would suggest, Doctor, that we dispose of this bothersome insect and be done with the matter. My organization has sunk far too much capital into this project to let an occurrence as minor as this get in our way at this stage of the operation."

"Of course, Mr. Pendergast," Irvine agreed solemnly. He poked at the immobile green form on the floor beside the Web-slinger with his toe. "And what about the Hulk?"

Pendergast examined the man-brute with distaste. "The Hulk has served his purpose, Dr. Irvine.

"Kill them both!"

Chapter 19

"Countdown at T minus ten minutes and counting."

Professor Abraham Warner's eyes went automatically to the digital clock on the console before him, confirming the publicly made announcement in the control room of the Niagara Falls complex with his own equipment.

"Begin final system check," he murmured into the microphone.

The rows of computer consoles in the low-ceilinged room were all occupied this morning before dawn, two days after the bizarre battle that had taken place in the large hangar beyond this room. Men and women, their faces bathed in the sickly green glow of the television screens, worked tensely, each performing their own highly specialized task.

The plate-glass observation window was gone, replaced by a giant rear-projection screen that showed an overhead view of the spacious hangar. The circular steel door in the floor was open, revealing a thirty-foot-deep well in which sat a fifty-foot-high booster rocket!

A high tower stood alongside the rocket, fuel and telemetry lines snaking from it, attached to the tall, glistening silver needle of metal. The ship carried no markings on its sleek skin. An equipment package sat atop the rocket, protected by detachable shields.

Technicians in orange-and-white jump suits hurried to complete their work in the hangar. Several small vehicles were parked around the pit.

Prof. Warner looked up at the screen and pressed a button on the console. The scene shifted instantly to a view from the bottom of the well, pointing up the length of the rocket. Billows of gas, liquid oxygen turning gaseous on contact with air as the ship's tanks were topped off, filled the pit. But through the white clouds could be seen two figures, seemingly chained to the body of the rocket over the triangular tail fins.

Warner pressed another button, bringing the view into close-up.

"Don't worry about our passengers, Abraham," a voice behind the bearded scientist chuckled. "They're not going anywhere."

Dr. Irvine stopped beside Warner's chair at the central control console and smiled at the picture on the screen before him. Spider-Man and Bruce Banner, both men apparently unconscious, were securely chained to the rocket.

"Isn't this a bit melodramatic, Daniel?" Warner asked with uncertainty.

"Nonsense, old friend. Where's your sense of humor gone?"

Warner's eyes flicked across the information on the screen before him. "I don't consider murder humorous," he said coolly.

"Then don't think of it as *murder,* my dear Professor," Irvine said with a smile. "Consider it a *necessity!*"

Abraham Warner stiffened in his seat. "I never knew you to be so *heartless*, Daniel," he said softly. "I thought life was important to you."

"Oh, but it *is*," Irvine assured him. "My life, at least."

The bearded scientist turned in his seat, regarding his colleague with pitying eyes. "Is it money that does this to you, Daniel?" he wanted to know.

Irvine laughed. "Don't go getting moralistic with me at this stage of the game, Abraham. Of course it's the money. It's why I'm here; it's why you're here!

"Look, Pendergast and his syndicate are paying good money for our talents, with a promise of much more to come *when* the project succeeds. That makes those two," he stabbed a finger toward the large screen, "a danger to everything we hope to get out of this. And don't think you're living the clean life yourself, good friend." The doctor patted Warner on the shoulder. "In case you've forgotten, what we're doing here is illegal. And when you consider that we do it to put us in a position to engage in espionage and blackmail on an international scale, well," he shrugged broadly and spread his hands before him, "I'm sure your imagination can fill in the rest!"

"T minus seven minutes, eighteen seconds and counting."

His cheeks red with anger, Prof. Warner turned back to his console.

"Don't take it like this," Irvine offered with a smile. "We both knew what we were getting into, didn't we?"

Warner did not answer.

"Good morning, gentlemen." Pendergast was smiling with genuine pleasure as he approached the two scientists, his cool gray eyes sparkling in the dim light of the control room. "Is all in readiness?"

"Good morning, Mr. Pendergast," Dr. Irvine said, returning the smile.

Warner nodded briskly, not looking up from his display screen. "Everything is proceeding as scheduled."

"Splendid!" the man in the expensively tailored suit said.

Prof. Warner was running through the final checklist with the technicians at the other consoles.

"T minus four minutes and counting."

"Fueling completed," Warner spoke into his mike. "Seal tanks."

"Latest weather conditions are A-okay for go signal," a voice said through the headphones.

"T minus two minutes and counting."

Warner said, "All systems are on automatic for go."

"All personnel clear the launch area. T minus one minute, thirty seconds."

"Retract tower," the scraggly bearded scientist ordered.

The lines leading from the launch tower to the rocket disengaged and the tower itself began to slide into the ground.

"T minus one minute and counting."

"All right, ladies and gentlemen," Warner said, speaking through his mike to all the technicians at their places. "This is it. Begin radar-scramble sequence alpha. Open launch ceiling."

As the hinged roof swung in on its hydraulic pumps, a device was activated on board the rocket to send out scrambling signals to any radar device that might pick it up on its flight into space.

"Thirty seconds and counting."

The ceiling was open, revealing the slowly brightening sky of the new day.

"On-board computer is go."

"Fuel mixture is go."

"T minus ten seconds. Nine."

Dr. Irvine clasped his hands behind his back and loosely crossed his fingers. "Good luck, Abraham," he said.

"Eight. Seven. Six."

"Begin ignition sequence," Warner said. He wiped away the perspiration that ran down the side of his face.

"Five. Four. Three."

"We have ignition!" a voice said through the headset. The clouds of billowing fumes were spilling from the launch well, filling the evacuated hangar as a deep rumble shook the control room from without.

"Two."

The rocket trembled on the pad.

"One. Lift-off!"

Almost imperceptively at first and then faster, the towering silver needle inched its way off the pad, gathering speed so slowly it seemed certain to topple before it could clear the launch well. But inches turned to feet and then yards as the rocket engines' boost increased. Then it was out of the pit and straining for the sky, through the open launch ceiling and then, finally, the open air.

A jubilant cheer swept through the control room as the rocket's earth-shaking rumble receded. Even Prof. Warner allowed himself a short smile of relief as he watched the rocket disappear into the gray dawn on the giant screen.

"And so it begins," Pendergast smiled.

"And ends," Irvine added. "For Spider-Man and the unfortunate Dr. Bruce Banner, that is."

The scientist chuckled happily to himself.

For a little more than three minutes, the rocket streaked through the early-morning sky, up through an atmosphere that grew thinner with each passing mile, until it was up into the stratosphere, gaining the speed necessary to break away from the Earth's gravitational pull.

The sky grew darker around the silver missile until nothing but the pitch-black vacuum of space surrounded it.

With a computer-relayed order from the Niagara Falls mission-control center, the main rocket engines shut down, their fuel reserves exhausted from its climb into space. Explosive bolts blew around the first stage and it disengaged smoothly from the rest of the ship. The cylinder spun lazily back toward Earth to disintegrate in the upper atmosphere.

Booster jets fired at an altitude of 400 miles and the second stage and shielded equipment package at its nose swung into orbit around the glowing green-blue marble far below.

Ninety minutes later, after completing a single orbit, the rockets fired once again, whipping the spacecraft out from its path about the planet.

The shields exploded automatically from the nose of the ship as it rose silently away from Earth. The exposed satellite shone dull black in the glare of the sun, at home in the frozen vacuum of outer space for the first time since it was created.

"Three seconds," Prof. Warner said.

His finger hovered over the red switch that would separate the microwave-transceiver satellite from the booster rocket.

"Now!"

His thumb jabbed the switch and sent a signal beaming 23,000 miles into space. The signal released a series of clamps that was holding the satellite to the booster ship and sent it spinning slowly into a fixed, permanent orbit directly above the Niagara Falls complex.

"Deploy solar screens."

Another command was flashed to the heavens that unfurled a pair of thin, golden wings from against the body of the satellite. They rolled out slowly and turned on well-lubricated rotors until they caught the bright sunlight across the full length of their surface.

Prof. Warner watched as the solar energy charged the satellite's internal batteries, the information flashing across his computer screen. At last he took a deep breath. "Okay," he said into his mike, his face tense. "Activating satellite systems. In sequence. Begin." His eyes shifted to a lone, unlit bulb in the center of the console. The color it glowed when it went on would determine success or failure.

The light blinked on.

Green.

Telemetry flowed across his screen from the activated satellite, each pulse of electronically encoded information bringing further assurance of a successful operation.

"Congratulations, Prof. Warner," Pendergast said. "It could not have gone smoother."

"Thank you," the scraggly bearded scientist exhaled softly. He pulled off his headset and sighed happily as he laid it on his console. "Now it's all possible," he said only half aloud.

"You've worked hard for this moment, Abraham," Dr. Irvine said. "You should be very proud."

"Yes, I am," Warner smiled. He glanced at his screen and his smile broadened. "Look," he said. "SpySat has established contact with its nearest neighbor in orbit, Western Electronics' EarthVue.

"Soon, EarthVue will set up a relay with *its* nearest neighbor, which in turn will bounce the maser beam to the next satellite and so on and so forth all around the planet until they are all linked together with SpySat at the center to form a vast web, a network that encircles the Earth.

"Intelligence data from the world over, international and national telephone, telex and telegraph communications, intelligence satellites, deep-space weather-observation stations—virtually every bit of knowledge and information broadcast or communicated today passes through at least one of the satellites we are now on line with.

"And it's all ours!"

"Free and clear and for sale," Pendergast smiled. "To any nation or individual who can pay our price. And, gentlemen," he said with a twinkle in his hard eyes, "it's a seller's market."

Chapter 20

A LOUD ROAR FILLED SPIDER-MAN'S EARS.
He shook his head to clear away the annoying
thundering that threatened to split his aching skull.
His head banged against metal.

The Web-slinger's eyes snapped open.

What the . . . ?

He was upright with his hands chained to his sides
and bound to a curving metal surface inside a deep,
brightly lighted pit that was alive with clouds of billowing, swirling gas. He was vibrating violently. . . .
No, the surface he was chained to was shaking with
the fury of powerful pent-up forces.

"Ten. Nine. Eight."

Spidey heard the words faintly through the deafening roar. *A countdown!*

*Considering what I know of their plans, that means
they're getting ready to launch their microwave doo-
hickey into orbit!*

And guess who made it on to the passenger list at the last minute!

Spider-Man strained against the chains, exerting as much power as he could muster. It wasn't enough.

Maybe these things will give eventually, but the old clock on the wall tells me I'm rapidly running out of any and all eventuallys!

"Two. One. Lift-off!"

The Wall-crawler flattened against the side of the rocket as the vibrations increased and the ship lifted off the launchpad. The engines' flaming exhaust spit from the roaring rockets and splashed back up from the asbestos pads to lick at the Web-slinger's legs.

His arms splayed to the sides as the rocket streaked through the open ceiling. His fingers touched flesh.

The Hulk! I'd forgotten about him! They must've gassed him too, and kept him gassed, otherwise he would've busted out of these chains like they were wet spaghetti by now!

Guess that means it's up to yours truly to pull our collective fat, green or otherwise, out of the fire!

Spider-Man found he had several inches of lateral movement in either direction with his hands. He began groping along the length of the chain he could reach. The wind whistled shrilly past his ears and the tug of increasing gravity pressed him painfully against the chain.

The rocket cleared the complex, heading toward the heavens and slightly south.

The Web-slinger's right hand brushed against a hard lump of metal dangling from the chain.

The padlock!

He tugged frantically on the chain, sliding it around until he could easily reach the lock. *At the rate this thing's climbing, I've got about five seconds before we'll be too high to make my busting out of this worth the hassle!*

Twisting his hand at an awkward angle, Spider-Man managed to jam the nozzle of his web shooter into the lock's keyhole. Even as he jabbed at the button in his

palm, he felt the lock being pushed out of his reach
by the mounting pressure.

It's now or never, Petey!

The thick web fluid gushed heavily into the lock
and filled the insides, pressing against the tumblers
with more and more pressure as the compressing fluid
sought release.

Come on, baby!

Snick!

The padlock snapped open and as he started to fall
away from the climbing rocket ship, Spider-Man swept
into action. In a single, fluid motion, he reached
around and grabbed the man hanging beside him.

His other hand flashed before him, shooting a
strand of webbing at the landscape streaking by a
quarter of a mile below.

*Now I better pray somebody up there still has some
kindly feelings left for me!*

The webbing snagged on the uppermost branch of a
tall, bare tree planted alongside a deserted highway.
Deep piles of snow had drifted around the thick tree
trunk or had been pushed there by snowplows clearing
the highway. Either way, it was just what the doctor
ordered.

Grasping the unconscious man tightly over his
shoulder, Spider-Man allowed himself to drop unchecked. *Who the hell is this? Unless the Hulk's lost
a couple of hundred pounds and developed a weird
rash all over his body, it looks like the mad scientists
have a grudge against more people than just me!*

Spider-Man and Bruce Banner were rushing at a
sickening speed toward the ground. Spidey held tight
to the single, narrow strand of webbing, tensing his
whole body for what was to happen next.

Suddenly, they were no more than twenty feet
above the treetop. Spider-Man released his guide-line
and shot out another, shorter strand of webbing. With
the ten-foot line grasped firmly in Spidey's hand, the
two men fell past the tree; then, with a sharp, agoniz-

ing jerk to the costumed youth's shoulder, they stopped.

Spider-Man yelled in pain and released the web instantly. They dropped into the deep drifts of snow piled about the tree.

Far above, the speeding rocket reached toward the heavens.

Chapter 21

SPIDER-MAN LAY FOR LONG MINUTES half buried in the slushy, melting snow, gulping in lungfuls of cold, invigorating air. His shoulder and back throbbed uncomfortably, but nothing, as far as the Web-slinger could tell, was broken or seriously damaged.

The other man groaned and struggled weakly from the snowbank.

"Where . . . where am I?"

"Wherever the heck it is, you're not alone, friend," Spidey said.

The two men pulled themselves from the deep snow and collapsed immediately on a dry patch of ground on the shoulder of the road.

Spider-Man rubbed his aching shoulder. He regarded his companion curiously. The man was relatively young and most frail looking. He was clad in the tattered remains of blue jeans.

155

"You must be a bit on the chilly side in that getup, mister," Spidey said. "Although there must be something to it, fashionwise that is. I met a guy by the name of the Hulk not too long ago who was wearing the same thing."

The brown-haired man buried his face in his hands. "The Hulk," he whispered miserably. "It's always the Hulk."

Spidey's face was puzzled beneath his mask. "How —" he began. He stopped abruptly as the man looked up at him. "Hey, you're Dr. Bruce Banner, aren't you? I recognize you from the picture on the back of your books!"

"*You've* read *my* books?" Bruce looked startled. "Perhaps there's something more to you than I've been led to believe, Spider-Man."

"Naw," the Wall-crawler shrugged. "I thought *A Study of Gamma-Ray Radiation and the Human DNA* was a travel guide and home fix-it book. Now," he added quickly, "would you mind telling me what the country's foremost expert on gamma rays was doing getting tied to rocket ships with erstwhile superheroes by a gaggle of gaga scientists?"

"You forget, Spider-Man," Bruce said sadly. "While I may be the foremost expert in my field, I'm also the Hulk."

Spidey slapped his hand to his forehead. "Jeez, am I stupid! Of course." He looked at the scientist. "So how'd the Hulk get involved in this?"

Bruce Banner shrugged. "That's just it," he said. "I don't know. I went to Chicago to see a Dr. Irvine at the Institute for Radiation Research and . . ."

"That's what it says on the signs at the complex."

"What?"

"Go ahead. I'll explain later."

Bruce Banner told Spider-Man everything he could recall, about changing to the Hulk at the airport in Chicago and coming to in a cell.

The young physicist slammed his fist angrily into the palm of his hand. "Except I have no idea what the

Hulk may've done for them," he said. "I don't remember anything after I changed.

"Now, how did I get here—and, more importantly, how did I get here with you?"

"Sit back and prepare to have your high IQ boggled, Doc," Spider-Man said. "You ain't gonna believe what you've just been through."

The Web-slinger started at the beginning, with the robbery in Manhattan. For the next fifteen minutes he told the astonished scientist everything he knew, changing only those details necessary to protect his alter ego.

When he was through with his story, Bruce Banner leaned back in wonder. "That's . . . incredible!" he gasped. "A private organization launching its own satellite into orbit without NASA or governmental permission or aid."

"I kind of doubt old Uncle Sam would be too thrilled offering help to the folks who are planning to blackmail him with his own secrets."

"Of course," Bruce said impatiently. He chewed on the inside of his cheek and stared off into the slowly brightening sky.

"We've got to stop them," Bruce Banner said at last. "We've got to smash this thing before it gets out of hand."

"Agreed. Only . . ." Spider-Man hesitated.

"What?"

"Well," the Wall-crawler said slowly. "It's not like I don't appreciate the offer, Doc, but truth to tell, you don't look like you'd be much . . . uh, good in a tussle."

Bruce grinned lopsidedly. "Wait until the action starts, my friend," he said. "*Then* you'll see how effective I can be."

"Touché." Spider-Man hauled himself to his feet. "It's just kind of tough remembering that beneath the mild, inoffensive exterior I see before me lies seven feet of angry Hulk."

Bruce Banner looked hard into Spider-Man's face.

"No," He shook his head. "It's really not all that difficult to remember, Spider-Man, once you've lived with
it long enough."

Spider-Man and Bruce Banner picked their way
through the thick underbrush several yards off the side
of the highway. The sun was high in the east, lighting
the clearing sky and bringing warmth to the new day.

Bruce led the way, stalking silently back toward the
complex on the bank of the Niagara River.

*What's with this guy, anyway? He hasn't said word
one since we started walking.*

But the slender young scientist was lost in thoughts
of his own; deep, black thoughts that caused his handsome face to cloud with anxiety. He did not seem to
notice the branches and thorns that scraped past his
naked chest and back.

Somehow, the Hulk had been instrumental in helping Irvine and his confederates launch that satellite
into orbit. They had tricked him, trapped him with a
carrot at the end of a stick and then put that uncontrollable part of his psyche to work on their foul deeds.

He had been used, damn it!

Bruce Banner clenched his fists in anger, venting his
anger by smashing aside the branches that blocked his
way. What the Hulk did on his own, through his own
brutish ignorance, was hard enough for the young scientist to live with. But when unscrupulous men har-
nessed that power for their schemes, it was worse—
far worse. Property demolished by his savage alter
ego could be replaced or rebuilt, but vital information
stolen from space could not, and it could lead to ir-
reparable damage—or the loss of life.

But it's not going to happen, Bruce swore to himself.
*If I have to tear down that place with my bare hands
to prevent it; so help me, I will!*

*We're probably getting close. I ought to warn
Doc. . . .*

Suddenly, Spider-Man's amazing spider-sense flared

to life. And even as it tingled through his skull, his ears pricked up.

Snap!

"Doc!" he whispered harshly.

Bruce turned. "What . . . ?"

"Shhh!" Spidey put a finger to his lips and pointed into the bushes at their side. "A little birdie just told me we've got some unexpected company headed this way."

Bruce stiffened.

"Who do you think it is?"

"Trouble, more than likely. We're awfully close to the base. They've probably got guards stationed around the perimeter to keep out anyone who comes sniffing around, curious about the big noises coming from around here."

"What do we do now?"

Spidey grinned under his mask. "Get rid of 'em. What else? You wait here, Doc. I want to save the Hulk for when he's got something else to batter around instead of *me*."

Bruce nodded tensely.

The Web-slinger ducked into the underbrush, his movement surprisingly quiet for his speed.

I don't know how many of them there are, but since when do I worry about the odds?

There were four of them in all, men dressed in the gray uniforms of the complex's security force and with small revolvers strapped unobtrusively to their belts. Two of the men walking through the thin woods carried walkie-talkies.

Guards it is. Give the man a cigar!

There's no chance of me and the doc making it back to the base without these clowns accidentally tripping over us, so, like I told the man, it's time to get rid of 'em!

"Yoo-hoo, boy scouts!" Spider-Man called as he stepped out from behind the cover of a thick tree.

The guards were stunned by the sight of the bizarrely costumed man suddenly appearing before them. That was just what the Wall-crawler was counting on.

He charged into the men, throwing himself full-length into the closely grouped quartet. They went down beneath him in a pile of gray-covered, flailing limbs. Spidey's fist connected with a jaw and one man tumbled over backward to lie unmoving in a patch of snow.

Spider-Man ducked under a clumsily thrown kick and grabbed the black-shoed foot by the ankle. He yanked up, twisting hard on the foot. The guard howled in surprise as he smacked face first into the hard ground.

The third guard grabbed Spider-Man from behind and wrapped his arms around the Wall-crawler's throat. The remaining man started toward the captive crime fighter, his clenched fist poised to strike.

"You're really a dreamer, friend," Spider-Man told him.

The Web-slinger threw himself forward, flipping the man holding him over his back.

"Yiii!" the hapless man screamed as he flew toward his companion. Both guards collided with a thud and sank to the ground.

"Okay, Doc," Spidey called into the underbrush.

Bruce Banner appeared between two bushes. He looked at the guards on the ground and then at Spider-Man, obviously impressed. "That couldn't have taken more than three or four seconds in all."

"That's what comes of practice," Spidey admitted modestly.

Bruce Banner allowed himself a smile. "It really isn't true what the papers say about you," he decided.

"That stuff about taking old ladies only halfway across the street and leaving them there? Heck, I haven't done that kind of thing in years."

"Okay. What's next?"

Spider-Man's arm swept out in an elaborate gesture. "Lead on, MacDuff."

As soon as the sound of the two men pushing

through the brush could no longer be heard in the clearing where the four men lay, one of the unconscious guards stirred.

He sat up and groggily rubbed a hand across his tender jaw. He shook his head and groped on the cold, hard ground for his walkie-talkie.

"Group Three reporting in," he said gingerly into the radio as he tried talking without moving his swollen jaw. "Group Three to Control."

"*Yeah, Group Three.*"

"Tell Mr. Pendergast—"

"Spider-Man's here?"

Pendergast was thunderstruck. His gray eyes narrowed and he jerked his head around from the radio to stare dangerously at Daniel Irvine.

"That . . . that's impossible," the scientist insisted. "Spider-Man's dead. He and Banner were smashed like insects on the rocket by the tremendous G force. They had to be!"

"Then *how,* Doctor," Pendergast asked in icy tones, "do you explain four guards being attacked and beaten by him?"

"They're mistaken!"

"*Really,* Dr. Irvine."

"But . . ."

"*Enough,* Doctor. We'll continue this discussion later. Alone." The tall man turned to Prof. Warner, seated at his control console. "Professor," he said. "We have Spider-Man's location pinpointed. Banner's probably still alive as well. Is it possible for you to lock the maser on them?"

Warner answered immediately. "Of course, Mr. Pendergast. The sensors can pinpoint a dime, let alone two men."

"Their interference is becoming increasingly dangerous to our work here, Prof. Warner. Do it!"

The bearded scientist swiveled around slowly in his seat, his face blanching as he suddenly understood the meaning of the steely-eyed man's words. "No," Warner breathed. "You *can't!*"

"But I can, Professor, and I *will!*" Pendergast hissed through clenched teeth.

"Use the maser and blast those meddling fools to ashes!"

Chapter 22

THE TREE IN FRONT OF BRUCE BAN-
ner split lengthwise as a ruby-red beam of light flashed
from the sky and touched the top of the tall trunk.

Even as the two halves fell to the ground, Spider-
Man grabbed the startled physicist around the waist
and pulled him to the ground.

"What the hell was *that?*" Bruce practically
screeched.

"Calm down, Doc. For all we know, it was just a
bolt of lightning."

"Lightning? There's not a cloud in the sky."

"So when did I say I knew anything about meteorol-
ogy?"

"Be serious, man!"

A second flash of ruby-red light caused the ground
a mere half dozen feet before them to explode in a
shower of soil and dirty snow.

"You want serious, Doc?" Spidey said. "Then try
this on for size: *run!*"

Like runners in a competition, the strange duo launched themselves to their feet and raced into the woods. Pencil-thin beams of ruby light stabbed from the sky above, tracing their path through the brush with its deadly blasts.

"I don't know how much longer I can go on," Bruce panted after several minutes. He was beginning to fall behind the Web-slinger.

"Don't think about it, Doc. Just remember what that laser or whatever it is did to the tree!" Spider-Man was running with much less effort, breathing in an even, steady rhythm.

Bruce Banner's heart pounded in his chest. He gasped in pain as a stitch tore through his side. He had to stop, had to catch his breath, if only for a moment. But a shower of cold dirt from the maser beam's closest blast urged him on in spite of the pain.

Suddenly, the maser stabbed into the ground before the two men. Spidey shoved Bruce roughly to one side while he threw himself in the opposite direction, avoiding the latest crimson beam that his spider sense had warned him would strike where he and Bruce Banner stood.

The maser beam seemed to lock on the Web-slinger, following his movements in an ever-tightening circle as Spider-Man leaped through a series of desperate acrobatics to avoid its deadly touch.

This is getting us nowhere—fast!

Spider-Man sent a strand of webbing flying toward a nearby tree and, as he swung over the small crater dug into the ground by the ruby light, he scooped Bruce Banner into his arms. Swinging in a wide arc, he let go of the webbing and both men dropped to the ground.

"After you, Alphonse," Spidey said.

"Right with you, Gaston," Bruce shouted as they started running once again.

Bruce discovered new reserves of strength somewhere inside of himself and found he could now keep pace with the agile Web-slinger and remain just ahead of the ruby-red beams. You can't let yourself get killed here, he told himself harshly.

But then the frail young scientist tripped over a rock and sprawled headlong on the ground.

"Doc!"

Spider-Man skidded to a stop and started to run back to his fallen companion. But the maser was firing with blinding speed now, ringing the helpless scientist with its lethal firepower. Bruce tried to rise as the ground exploded beside his leg.

"No!" he screamed.

His heart pounded in his chest as the blood pounded in his throbbing temples, Bruce rose to one knee. The flashes of red seemed to merge into a single crimson haze.

Fssstt!

The maser beam washed over the man called Bruce Banner in the next instant, but the ruby-red light seemed to splash harmlessly off his broad, emerald back.

The Hulk roared his rage at the pain that seared across his back and swiped his powerful jade hands through the intangible beams.

"Arrggh!" he bellowed as the lights would not break but merely sent new flashes of white-hot pain coursing through him.

Hoo-boy!

Spider-Man had stepped back in surprise, watching with eyes staring in astonishment as Bruce Banner underwent the most amazing metamorphosis the Wall-crawler had ever witnessed. *I was afraid this was going to happen! I had hoped it would've held off until we needed the Hulk's strength!*

Then again, considering the Hulk's the first thing I've seen that those beams can't demolish, I guess we need him more than I thought.

Now I've gotta hope he believes me when I tell him I'm on his side!

"Bah!" the man-monster huffed. "Lights do not make any sense. They can touch Hulk but Hulk can-

not touch them." The green giant crouched, readying
to leap away from this baffling attack.

"Hulk! *Wait!*" Spider-Man called.

The Hulk turned and then grunted as another flash
of ruby red splashed across his barrel chest and drove
him to the ground. The beams streaked across the
length of the Hulk's body before moving on toward
Spider-Man.

"Hulk, listen to me," the Wall-crawler pleaded with
the great green man. The Hulk struggled to his feet,
his emerald eyes glazed with pain. He shook his head
like a wet dog and growled.

The Wall-crawler somersaulted out of the maser's
range, bouncing across the ground to the Hulk.

"We've gotta get out of here, Hulk! *Quick!*"

"Huh? Hulk remembers you, bug-eyes. You tried
to . . . hurt Hulk!"

"You've got it all wrong, big buddy," Spidey said
quickly, his eyes drawn to the flashes of crimson light
tearing a path of destruction toward them. "I'm your
friend, Hulk. *Friend!*" he repeated, just to make sure
the man-monster got the message. "I'm not the one
who's trying to hurt you. See?" The Web-slinger
pointed to the approaching maser beam. "It's the
other men, the ones in the white coats who are trying
to kill you *and* me. That means we're on the same
side. Me friend, them enemy!"

*Lord, I hope this green turkey can follow a little
bit of simple logic, because if he doesn't, my goose is
cooked either way. Either the Hulk grabs my legs and
makes a wish or he leaves me here to get fried by
that Buck Rogers death ray!*

The Hulk pondered this for what seemed to Spider-
Man to be an eternity before his primitive face relaxed into a smile. The jade giant clapped a friendly
hand on Spidey's shoulder, almost knocking the Wall-
crawler to the ground with his enthusiastic camara-
derie.

"Yes," the Hulk proclaimed. "Bug-eyes is Hulk's
friend."

Spider-Man breathed a sigh of relief.

A second later, the maser beam was tearing up the ground at his feet, reminding the Web-slinger that he was not yet in the clear.

"Okay, buddy," he shouted. "Let's fly this burg!"

The Hulk crouched and Spider-Man jumped up onto the man-monster's broad back. With a leap, they were airborne.

Spidey clung tightly to the emerald colossus' neck as they soared in a high arc, the Hulk's seemingly casual leap carrying them a quarter of a mile from the maser blasts. The green-skinned behemoth came down, his thick legs bending to absorb the impact of landing and then sprang back into the sky.

Cripes! We're heading away from the base!

Unless . . . yeah, Doc Banner said the Hulk doesn't retain any of his memory and vice versa. I should've pointed!

The Web-slinger realized from the queasy feeling in his stomach that they were once again falling to the ground. He glanced down to see where they were. And if the sight of the ground rushing up toward him at a dizzying speed wasn't enough to make Spidey's mouth stretch into a sick, grim line beneath his mask, the place they were about to land in was.

I was afraid of this!

During the winter months, the city of Niagara Falls, New York could almost be described as a quiet little upstate resort town, closed for the off-season and empty of tourists.

Almost. For a look at the streets of Niagara Falls reveals something about the small city: the garish signs over souvenir ships lining the thoroughfares, the neon glowing coldly even in the light of day, the gaudy tourist attractions; the tacky look and feel of a city that feeds off itself in the name of tourism.

And, in truth, tourists still came to the city in the cold of winter. There were the young marrieds who

believed the falls were still the honeymoon capital of
the nation, or who could afford no better. There
were the familes who came for winter vacation to tour
the feature that made this small city on the US—
Canadian border the highly touted attraction it had
become: Niagara Falls.

There were no tourists on the streets in the center
of the city's small downtown area this early in the
morning, but a score of residents on their way to work
were about to witness perhaps the most bizarre occurrence in the city's colorful history.

A large figure appeared high in the sky and hurtled
like an out-of-control missile toward the streets below. It fell to the asphalt street in their midst as they
ran, fearful for their lives, out of its way. But it wasn't
a missile. It was a snarling, green giant with a lithe
young man in a dark-blue-and-red costume clinging
to his back.

A woman screamed and pushed frantically past her
husband as she ran for the safety of a nearby store.

There was no other sound in the still of the morning, save for the distant rumble of the mighty falls
and the heavy breathing of the Hulk as he glowered
at the people in the street with veiled, suspicious eyes.

"Easy, big buddy," Spider-Man said gently, patting
the big green man's back in reassurance.

"What is this place, bug-eyes?"

"A tourist trap, if you must know."

The Hulk stared blankly at Spider-Man.

"Forget it, big guy," the Wall-crawler said. "We
may not be doing any good to the townies here, but I
think we're pretty safe here until we start back t . . ."

FssssstttBAHWHOOOM!

A ruby-red needle of light pierced the air and
blasted through the sidewalk to their side.

I hadda open my big mouth, didn't I?

The Hulk roared his disapproval at this turn of
events. "Go away from Hulk, light!"

"Nice try, Greensleeves," Spidey breathed. "But

nobody's buying it. You've got to jump us out of here again."

"No. Hulk is tired of running away from lights."

"C'mon, this'll only be the second time."

The man-brute snarled at the sky. "Hulk does not run away from lights or anything else anymore. Hulk is staying!

And Hulk fights!"

The Hulk loped over to the bubbling pit created by the maser beam. He turned his face to the sky and awaited the next blast with fists clenched and snarling in defiance.

The green Goliath did not have to wait long.

A slender finger of light reached from the sky and burst across the Hulk's chest. The maser beam washed over him and forced the big green man down on one knee.

"You big, stupid . . . !" Spider-Man growled to himself as he ran to the Hulk's side. *That idiot'll keep standing there until that thing turns him into one big strip of overfried bacon!*

Spidey slammed into the Hulk's back as hard as he could. Weakened by the searing heat of the masers, the emerald colossus fell to the ground and rolled out from under the deadly fire.

"Hulk . . . thought bug-eyes . . . was his friend," the Hulk grumbled weakly. "Wh . . . does bug-eyes . . . attack Hulk?" The giant seemed wounded by the Wall-crawler's action.

"Nothing personal, big guy," Spidey assured him in a hurry. "But you can't fight these things like this. We've got to smash this beam at the source."

"Hulk is not afraid of stupid lights!"

"Maybe you're not, Greenie," Spider-Man said. "On the other hand, it's not afraid of you either. And considering it can kill you while you can't touch it, I think we'd better get out of here."

"Hulk can smash!"

"Not here, friend," the Web-slinger said.

The street to their right exploded.

"But I know where we can go where you can smash to your little green heart's content."

The Hulk's angry scowl turned into a savage smile.

"Okay, bug-eyes," the man-brute said. "Hulk will follow you."

Chapter 23

THE INCREDIBLE HULK TOOK TO THE SKY.

His leap carried him and a slightly nervous Spider-Man over the dingy wooden-frame storefronts to a residential street several blocks over. The maser beam tracked its prey from its perch 23,000 miles up in space. With uncanny mechanical accuracy, the maser aboard SpySat traced an exact line behind the flying Hulk, its deadly beam piercing pencil-thin holes through rooftops and streets.

Thoomp!

The Hulk landed and turned. He roared in anger when he saw the lethal light still behind him and closing fast. In quick succession, the maser beam sliced through the awning over a porch, the stairs of the same house, the front lawn, the sidewalk and a car.

Fahwooomsshh!

The ruby red-hot beam ignited the volatile fuel in

the car's tank. The automobile burst into a flaming ball of heat and sound and Spider-Man ducked behind the Hulk's thick, broad back for protection from the shower of shattered glass and flaming metal shards that followed.

The green Goliath swept Spider-Man into his arms and took to the air, the maser beam pursuing them relentlessly over the streets of Niagara Falls.

As they descended to the streets, Spider-Man spotted an elderly man shuffling obliviously from a luncheonette, zipping along at a surprising clip with his white walking stick tapping the ground before him.

Oh-oh! Hulk's going to put down next to that old man. . . .

The sidewalk beneath the Hulk's feet exploded as he was landing. The man-monster hit the smoldering asphalt at an awkward angle and lost his balance. As he fell, he threw Spider-Man clear, just as the ground next to the Hulk vaporized in an eruption of dust.

Snarling, the jade-hued giant pounded both of his massive fists into the sidewalk, splitting the concrete for fifteen feet in either direction.

But the maser beam was following Spider-Man as he rolled across the street, heading uncontrollably, thanks to the Hulk's careless throw, toward the old man. "Get out of the way!" the Wall-crawler screamed. The old man kept walking straight into the hail of deadly fire.

Damn! He must be deaf as well as blind!

Still rolling, Spidey twisted into a somersault while simultaneously firing a strand of webbing at a nearby lamp post. He pulled himself from the ground and swung in a high arc, the ruby-red beams only inches behind him. He swept past the old man and scooped him gently from the ground. Spidey swung back and deposited the struggling old man in a recessed doorway.

"Sorry about the rough treatment, old timer," he apologized even though he was fairly certain he could not be heard. "But the alternatives would've been a whole heck of a lot worse!"

Spider-Man jumped to the ground and took off on a run toward his giant green companion. The Hulk, unable to unleash his anger on the streamers of light stalking him from the heavens, was venting his awesome rage on the streets of Niagara Falls. His powerful hands tore up ragged hunks of concrete and sent them hurtling through the air.

This is getting totally out of hand. So far we've been lucky and nobody's been killed . . . yet! But that old man back there proves that luck can't hold up much longer!

The Hulk hefted a man-sized hunk of concrete over his head as a makeshift shield, but the powerful maser shattered it to rubble.

"Hulkie baby," the Web-slinger shouted as he leaped onto the big green man's shoulder. "It's time we cut the clowning around and smashed this thing once and for all!"

"Hulk will go now," the man-monster agreed reluctantly. "But there better be something for Hulk to smash . . . *soon!*"

"Fear not, jolly green giant. I've got a rocket-launch site in mind you're gonna just love!"

Pendergast bent anxiously over Prof. Warner's shoulder, his cold gray eyes searching the complex control console before the bearded scientist. His lean, handsome face was taut in the dim green light of the screen and beads of perspiration dotted his forehead.

"What's happening, Professor?" he demanded tensely.

Warner shrugged, his eyes scanning the series of green letters that crawled rapidly across his screen. "I—I'm not entirely certain."

"Has the maser beam gotten them yet or not?"

"It's . . . no. No, the beam is still on automatic search and fire." Warner shook his head. "It's remarkable, but somehow they're avoiding the maser."

Pendergast straightened slowly. "I know you don't approve of this, Prof. Warner, but I warn you, if you're deliberately screwing this up and letting those meddlers escape, I'll . . ."

"No!" Warner insisted. "We never anticipated using the maser on such small, fast-moving targets. You realize that Spider-Man is an exceptionally agile man. With his remarkable reflexes, he could conceivably avoid the beam for as long as his stamina holds out. And as for the Hulk—well, frankly, I'm not even certain how effective, if at all, it will be against his supertough skin."

The slender man clenched his fists at his sides. "I do not like this, Professor," he said sharply. "I do not like this at all! If Spider-Man and the Hulk are not disposed of immediately, the future of this entire project is in serious jeopardy."

"I know . . ." Prof. Warner started.

He stopped suddenly, his words lost under the thundering shudder that ran through the entire building. He looked up at Pendergast, his eyes shiny with fear. "An explosion," the professor whispered hoarsely.

Pendergast reached across the startled scientist and stabbed a finger at a button on the console. "Sounds like it came from the hangar."

The large view screen on the wall lit up, showing the men and women in the control room a high-angle view of the massive hangar beyond the room.

What they saw made them stop their work, staring in awe at the screen.

The steel doors in the ceiling were hanging from their hydraulic hinges, smashed open as if by a great explosion. But, when Pendergast zoomed the camera in for a shot of the two figures standing in the center of the hangar floor, he knew that explosives and bombs were the last things in the world he would have to worry about.

Especially now that Spider-Man and the Hulk were there!

Pendergast swore loudly and slammed his fist on the console.

"What should we do, Mr. Pendergast?" Warner's voice was quivering, a pathetic whine in the stunned silence of the control room.

"Turn off the maser," he shouted. "We don't want to blast ourselves! Then seal off the hangar. Get every available man in there and *stop* them, do you hear?

"Here we are, Hulkie," Spider-Man said, his arms spread wide to take in the entire hangar.

The big green man looked down at the strangely garbed man at his side.

"I said it's all yours, big fella. Start smashing away."

"Hulk can smash . . . *all* this, bug-eyes?" the emerald colossus asked uncertainly.

"Yep," Spidey nodded.

The Hulk's laugh rumbled deep in his broad chest as he ambled happily over to the closest wall. Feet planted wide, he regarded the thick concrete with pleasure.

The Hulk sent a massive green fist crashing through the wall and ripped loose huge chunks of concrete and steel reinforcement rods as he withdrew his hand. Holding the twisted debris out in his hand for Spidey's inspection, he said, "Like this?"

Spider-Man nodded his approval. "That's the ticket, cutie. Now let's see if you can break the Olympic record for building demolition, okay?"

Grinning happily, the Hulk dropped what was in his hand and turned back to his wall.

Who would've thought it? Old green eyes is nothing but a big, dumb, albeit incredibly strong kid at heart! Even though he's in the process of tearing down a forty-foot-high concrete bunker, he acts more like a little boy with a brand-new toy than a monster.

A steel door at the far end of the hangar rolled open and twenty men, some in the gray guards' uniforms, others in bright-orange jump suits, rushed out. They swarmed toward the Web-slinger, several of them armed.

Ah, it would seem the time has come for me to do my thing!

Chapter 24

SPIDER-MAN'S GLOVED HANDS CLOSED around the pistol in the guard's hand as his other hand shot out to deliver a stinging blow to the man's chin. The guard tumbled backward, and, before the Web-slinger could see where he landed, two more men were on him.

He rammed his elbow into the first man's throat and ducked easily beneath the other's fist. Spidey gathered the front of the man's jump suit in his fist and yanked the wide-eyed technician toward him while bringing his knee up into the man's stomach. The orange-suited man gasped, a sound that turned to a scream when the Web-slinger lifted him off the floor.

Spidey tossed the man through the air and sent him sprawling into a group of three others. The Wall-crawler spun around as he felt a punch glance off his shoulder. *Fun is fun, but I can't waste time fighting*

the hired help. That satellite and the death ray are be-
ing controlled from somewhere in here, I'm sure of it!
And that's what I've got to find!

Three men rushed at Spider-Man at once. He
waited until their hands were about to close on him
before crouching and leaping straight up into the air.
He somersaulted over their heads and landed behind
his attackers.

Spidey's hand chopped down on a neck, then swung
back and backhanded another across the small of his
back. He planted his foot firmly against the third
man's rump and shoved him forward.

Then, without pausing for breath, he fired his webbing, at the ruined ceiling and pulled himself quickly
out of his attacker's reach. He swung himself forward,
high over their heads, zig-zagging madly along to
avoid the bullets that now whistled past him.

Meanwhile, the Hulk was tearing a large wedge of
concrete from the wall. He spun with it in his massive
hands and tossed the half ton of steel and concrete
at the guards like a great discus.

"Heads up!" one man screamed and they scattered
as the giant slab flew toward them.

"Ha!" the Hulk rumbled. "Look at puny men running from Hulk. They try to stop Hulk, but Hulk will
show them because Hulk is stronger than any man!

"Hulk is the strongest one there is!"

Nobody bothered to dispute the man-monster's
claim.

The guards and technicians stalked the growling
green Goliath with caution, shuffling toward him with
guns and clubs held at the ready. Snarling his contempt, the Hulk pounded one foot on the floor. The
ground shook as if caught in the grip of an earthquake,
throwing the guards off their feet.

The green behemoth leaped easily over the fallen
men and landed beside the metal covering over the
launch well. He crouched and dug his hands under
the inch-thick steel and tugged. The metal groaned
mournfully as it was peeled back like the lid of a sar-

dine can. Then, swinging around his thick torso, the
Hulk tore the thirty-foot-wide cover from the floor.

The Hulk dug his fingers into the steel and charged
at the wall with the cover held before him like a battering ram.

The thick wall crumbled like papier-mâché under
the assault, giving way to a smaller chamber alongside the hangar. The Hulk tossed aside the buckled
steel cover and attacked the remainder of the wall
with his bare hands. Chunks of concrete flew through
the air.

Pa-ting! Pa-ting!

Heavy-caliber bullets flattened harmlessly against
the man-monster's broad back. With a hunk of the
wall clutched in his hands, the Hulk whirled, snarling.
Three men stood a dozen feet from him, firing point-
blank.

The Hulk threw the piece of wall at them. The
armed men scattered as the block shattered on the
ground where they had stood a moment before.

"Puny men better leave Hulk alone," he raged. "Or
Hulk will smash men like Hulk smashes building!"

As if to punctuate his bellowed threat, the Hulk
pounded his hands into the floor, ripping up a length
of flooring material and whipping it through the air
like a carpet. Those unfortunate enough to be standing
on that particular piece of the floor found themselves
likewise whipped into the air, flying with limbs flapping like rag dolls.

The man-monster stood motionless in the center of
the room for several seconds with his dull, brutish
eyes flicking across the room searching for his next
target. Once located, he loped over to it and happily
continued his mindless rampage of destruction.

Dr. Daniel Irvine mopped at his glistening forehead
with a moist handkerchief as he watched the view
screen on the wall of the control room. Indeed, every-
one not engaged in vital operations of the orbiting
SpySat were staring in disbelief at what they saw.

The Hulk had jumped down into the exposed launch well and was busily demolishing it. Every bit of equipment he could wrap his great, green hands around was torn from the bottom of the thirty-foot pit. Steel and cement pads, massive exhaust funnels, fuel and telemetry lines, steel braces, all went flying out of the well. The debris spun through the air before crashing and clanging back to the floor.

"God help us," Dr. Irvine whispered in a mixture of fear and awe.

Pendergast glanced sharply at the scientist. "Can't you do something, Irvine?"

"Me?" Irvine's answer was punctuated with a shrill giggle. "Whatever in the hell do you think *I* can do about the monster?"

"You did it once before, Doctor!"

"Yes, and I could do it again—provided you deliver him unconscious to the isolation chamber so I can implant another control device in his ear!" The scientist was verging on hysteria as he watched the giant man-monster destroy everything he had worked to help create. He twisted the soaking handkerchief in his trembling hands. "Spider-Man knocked the damned thing out!"

Prof. Warner sat with his eyes glued to the view screen while he listened passively to the frantic reports coming in over his earphones. The complex was falling apart around them. The guard force had fled when the Hulk had begun tossing the wreckage about the hangar. But the bearded scientist was strangely calm despite all that was happening. He knew this endeavor was finished, shattered to a smoldering pile of rubble by a giant green monster and his bizarrely garbed companion, yet this fact did not bother him. Warner knew it should. After all, three years of his life were invested in the microwave transceiver and SpySat's delivery system.

But it just didn't matter anymore. Not SpySat, not the microwave device, not Pendergast and his omnipresent-yet-unseen investors.

Not anything. It was merely a matter of time.

"Professor!" Pendergast barked. "There must be something you can do?"

"I'm an old man," Abraham Warner sighed. "I can't go out there and fight the thing with my bare hands."

"Damn it," Pendergàst screamed, his cool, professional facade beginning to crumble as rapidly as the walls outside the control room were crumbling under the Hulk's fists.

"What kind of bumbling morons am I dealing with? How can you both just stand there and let those . . . those *freaks* destroy everything we've worked for?"

"What do you expect us to do, Pendergast?" Dr. Irvine snapped. "You and your people planned and built this installation, not us! If there are no provisions to handle trouble like this, *we* aren't the ones to blame. Not us."

Pendergast rested his clenched fists on top of Prof. Warner's console, squeezing shut his eyes against the painful glare from the view screen. "All right," he said slowly through tightly clenched teeth. "This is no time to get at each other's throats and panic. We must remain calm. Think this problem out logically."

Dr. Irvine shoved his hands into the deep pockets of his lab coat, bitterly regarding the giant green monster on the screen.

"Fine, Mr. Pendergast. *You* try logic on . . . that!"

The Hulk clambered out of the launch well, a twenty-foot length of the mangled launch tower trailing from his hand. Pleased with the havoc he had wreaked, the jade giant dropped the twisted steel tower back into the pit. There was still much to be done.

"Bug-eyes said Hulk should smash it *all*," he grumbled solemnly.

The green giant leaped up toward the partially ruined steel ceiling and grabbed hold of the twisted, metal launch door. He tore it loose from its partially covered hinges and followed it down to the floor forty feet below.

The Hulk landed heavily and bounded over to another wall. His fists punched through to the outside and then he was roaring like a crazed animal and tearing massive pieces from the steel-reinforced structure.

After several minutes of this, the green-skinned behemoth stepped back, panting heavily and surveying his handiwork.

Then, with a final blow to the decimated wall, the Hulk turned his back to it and set off in search of further whole things that he could reduce to little pieces.

Kreee-eek . . .

The Hulk looked over his shoulder.

The steel-reinforced wall groaned as, suddenly, two of the walls supporting what was left of the ceiling and severely weakened by the Hulk's pounding fists, collapsed under the weight. Steel and concrete rained down on the floor, clattering and crashing as they fell. The remaining portion of ceiling tilted, hanging suspended by several beams before breaking loose and falling to the ground, bringing down the entire far side of the huge hangar.

The Hulk watched this final destruction from the opposite side of the room. Even as the tons of debris crashed to the floor in a shower of dust, his brutish face twisted into a savage smile of pleasure, and he laughed.

"Ha! Hulk likes that!"

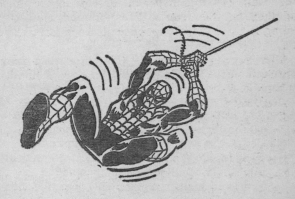

Chapter 25

Normally, I hate to leave a friend to handle that kind of trouble by himself, but . . . The amazing Spider-Man looked down to the floor of the hangar where the Hulk was busy swatting aside a group of armed security men. *Well, let's just say ol' Green-eyes seems to be able to take care of himself without any help from yours truly.*

Spider-Man began crawling along the ruined ceiling toward the door that had remained open after letting the guards into the hangar. He quickly lowered himself on his webbing and swung through the open doorway and into a long, well-lit corridor.

The Web-slinger dropped lightly to the polished metal floor and looked around. In the hangar beyond the corridor he heard the sounds of the Hulk's rampage of destruction but in here there was silence. Three doors were set on either side of the corridor, with a seventh door at the far end.

How come Monty Hall's never around when you really need him?

He stepped lightly over to the nearest door and pressed his ear against it. *Nada!*

The next three doors proved equally disappointing and, as the Wall-crawler headed for the next one in line, his head began to tingle a warning.

Now what?

Spider-Man turned to find himself face-to-face with the security guards and orange-clad men who were retreating into the corridor away from the Hulk. The man in the lead, a guard with a pistol grasped in his hand, saw the Web-slinger first and stumbled to a halt.

"Hey," the man yelled. "There's the other one!"

"Hiya, kiddies. What's the matter, doesn't little Hulkie want to play with you guys anymore?"

A dark-haired man in a jump suit leaped from the group and leveled his gun at Spidey. "Yeah? Let's see if *this* one can be shot!"

"Oh, I can be shot, all right," Spider-Man nodded.

Bang!

Spider-Man leaped up, his fingers sticking to the ceiling as he hauled himself from the bullet's path.

"But first, one of you dummies is gonna have to learn how to shoot straight." He dropped from the ceiling and landed on top of the closely-grouped men, his gloved fists swinging. He felt his hand connect with bone while he kicked another man's legs out from under him. He spun around and slammed his hand against a uniformed chest and shoved. Spidey whirled again and chopped another man across the bridge of his nose before grabbing an arm swinging a gun butt at his head and twisting it hard behind the owner's back. The man howled in pain and fell to the floor where another guard tripped over him and smacked his head against the hard floor.

Despite the Wall-crawler's strength, the overwhelming number of men was threatening to drag him down. Hands plucked at his costume and arms. *No good.*

I've got to extract myself from this mess and take on these slobs on firmer ground!

Suddenly, Spider-Man relaxed, allowing himself to be pulled down as he curled his lithe body into a tight ball. Shouting and swearing, the guards swarmed over him, throwing themselves in a pile over the Wall-crawler's body like a football team on their opponent's ball carrier.

Spidey tensed beneath the pile of bodies and, just as suddenly, exploded upright, throwing the men off him. He jumped to the wall and scampered to the ceiling where he hung upside down by his toes and fingers. The men were already staggering to their feet, looking around for the Web-slinger. Half a dozen of them, however, remained sprawled on the floor, unconscious.

Not a bad start, Web-head. Now that you've set yourself up with a neat little split, let's see if you can score a spare by knocking over the rest of these pinheads!

The Wall-crawler waved to the men below. "Yoo-hoo, boys. Up here! Sheesh, you guys are really awful at hide-and-seek, y'know?"

He fired a thick blanket of webbing at them. Four of the men dove out from under the falling net before they could be ensnared beneath it. All the others, however, were trapped, trying to fight their way free of the thick, sticky substance. Spider-Man dropped to the floor to deal with the remaining men.

"Okay, friends," he said lightly. "We've fooled around with these kid games long enough. It's time to get serious." He started walking toward them. "I challenge all of you to a game of Scrabble at ten paces!"

The only one of the four in a guard's uniform rushed at Spider-Man, his gun raised over his head like a club.

"Ah-ha. I see you *accept* my challenge." Spidey sidestepped the guard's clumsily swung club and lashed out his fist to chop down hard on the man's shoulder. With a howl of pain, the man stumbled forward. "Okay, here are the rules: you guys are supposed to try to bash my face down my throat while *I*—," Spider-Man said as he dropped the man with a right jab.

"—*Scrabble* your brains."

Spider-Man turned back to the others. They had spread out, one man to his right, a second to his left and the third directly in front of him.

And he's the one I've got to watch out for! He's almost as big as Greensleeves and twice as ugly!

The man before him was big, well over six feet tall with a barrel chest and thick, muscular arms. The two men at his sides moved in first, feinting with their hands as if making a grab for the Wall-crawler's arms. *Hey, if that's what they want, who am I to deny them their pleasure?*

Spidey allowed the man on his right to latch hold of his wrist and then, a moment later, the man on his left did likewise.

The tall man before him grinned in evil pleasure as he walked toward Spider-Man, pounding one large fist into his palm.

"This is going to be a real pleasure, weirdo," he breathed.

Spider-Man smiled to himself as he said, "A fundamental rule of the hero game, gentlemen, is the use of the bad guy's own evil intentions against him."

The man planted his feet firmly in front of the spread-eagled Spider-Man. "Sounds like you do that by boring them to death!"

"On the contrary, muscles, I do it by taking advantage of their stupidity."

Spider-Man swung his arms together before him, swinging the two men who held him together with a sickening sound of bone crunching against bone.

The big man seemed to loom over him now and Spider-Man dropped the others to the floor and threw a hard right into the man's stomach. The man grunted but still fell toward him with outstretched arms reaching for the Wall-crawler's throat. The Web-slinger leaned out of the way and swung his right fist into the man's jaw with a force that snapped the man's head back. One of his muscular arms wrapped around Spidey's neck and dragged the Web-slinger to the floor.

Spider-Man rolled out from beneath the big man but did not seem able to break his choking stranglehold. The Wall-crawler pounded on the man's neck with his fist several times before the form went slack, releasing his grip.

Breathing hard, Spider-Man got to his feet. With scarcely a glance at the trapped or unconscious men on the floor, he turned his attention to the remaining doors.

There was nothing until he came to the one at the end of the corridor.

He could dimly make out the sound of people and electronic gear behind the solid-steel sliding door. There was no knob or keyhole anywhere on the flat surface, just a glass plate set into the wall beside it with the outline of a palm print etched in black on it. Spidey pressed his palm to the plate and waited. Nothing happened.

Don't tell me you were really expecting it to work for you, Mr. Parker?

He stared thoughtfully at the door, the final obstacle between him and the destruction of the deadly satellite orbiting the Earth.

"Ah-*hah!*" he exclaimed suddenly and rushed back to where the fallen guards lay. The Web-slinger hefted one man in an orange jump suit over his shoulder and took the unconscious man back to the sealed door to the control room. He braced the limp man against the wall and pressed his hand to the steel plate.

The door slid open with a soft mechanical sigh.

Spider-Man allowed the unconscious man to slide to the floor and ran into the room.

All heads turned at the sound of the door opening. They had to tear their eyes from the view screen where the Hulk could be seen turning away from an outside wall that had seen better days just an instant before the roof gave way and tumbled to the floor, knocking out the cameras. The screen went black at the same moment Spider-Man heard the thundering roar of the collapsing hangar and felt the building shake.

"I think that means the jig's up, ladies and gents," Spider-Man announced.

Pendergast took a step forward from the control console, his handsome features contorted in a look of rage. "Not in the least, Spider-Man," he spat. "There are still guards and . . ."

Spidey jerked his thumb over his shoulder. "Not anymore, good-looking. I just finished sending them all off to a place very far away from here called sleepy land."

Pendergast swung back to face Prof. Warner and Dr. Irvine, his cold gray eyes flashing madly, seeking help. "The maser," he said quickly. "Use the maser, Warner!"

"Are you insane?" the bearded scientist exclaimed as he recoiled from the tall man in horror. "You don't seriously expect me to turn the maser on myself!"

"Use it, damn you!" Pendergast screamed and lunged at the console. His tightly clenched fists pounded at the controls, frantically searching for the button that would end the threat of the Web-slinger and his monstrous companion once and for all.

Spider-Man charged across the room and yanked the hysterical man away from the console. He threw Pendergast to the floor and planted himself between the man and the control console. "Cool it, fancy pants!"

Pendergast struggled to his knees, tugging at his tie. "Get him, damn your eyes," he screamed to the stunned, seated technicians. "Kill him before he ruins everything!"

"Mister," Spidey shook his head in disgust, "you're starting to get on my nerves." His gloved fist cracked against Pendergast's jaw, knocking the man to the floor, senseless.

He turned at the sound of feet running toward him and fired his webbing at the two technicians rushing at him. The web fluid wrapped tightly around their ankles and they crashed to the floor.

"I don't advise anybody else trying that," Spidey warned the rest of them. "Next time, I'm liable to forget myself and hurt somebody." He turned to study Prof. Warner's control panel. "What I *would* do, though, is hightail it out of here as fast as my little legs could carry me, 'cause as soon as I figure out what's what on this furshlugginer thing, I'm gonna do my darnedest to finish off the work started by my big green friend."

Nobody moved.

Spider-Man started to speak but was interrupted by Prof. Warner brushing by him. "Listen to him," the bearded scientist yelled. "It's over for us here. Finished! Get out!"

The Web-slinger looked at the scientist with surprise.

"I am a realistic man, Spider-Man," Warner said softly.

"And what about you, Doc?" Spidey asked Irvine.

The scientist clutched the soaking handkerchief in his hands. He glared with hate-filled eyes at the costumed youth. "Are you giving me a choice?"

Spider-Man shook his head.

Dr. Irvine turned on his heels and joined the procession of men and women rushing from the control room through an exit across the room.

Spidey's hand hovered uncertainly over the control console. "How does this work, Doc?" he asked Prof. Warner as the bearded scientist walked slowly to the exit.

Warner stopped and turned around. "You're going to destroy my satellite," he said simply.

"I can't leave it up there."

The professor shook his head and started walking again. "I said I was realistic, Spider-Man," he said without looking back. "But I can't help you. I won't try to stop you, but I can't tell you how to destroy three years' worth of my life's work." Within seconds, Spidey was alone in the control room.

He scanned the console. *Sheesh! I wonder which one of these turns on the automatic coffee maker?*

What the hey! Life's no fun if you don't take a chance every once in a while!

The Web-slinger jabbed at buttons on the console. Words flashed across the screen in front of him, but, as far as Spider-Man could see, nothing else happened. *C'mon, man, you've had enough training in computers in school to be able to figure out at least some of this gobbledygook!* He flipped switches and twisted dials and, suddenly, new information crawled rapidly across the screen and Spidey looked it over carefully. *Now this is more like it! If I read this right, the satellite's on a standby mode, ready to fire as soon as the target coordinates are fed into it!*

The Web-slinger's fingers flew across the computer keyboard, typing out information to be radioed 23,-000 miles into space. *I just hope to God I know what I'm doing!*

Beep! Beep! Beeeeep!

A screeching alarm sounded throughout the deserted control room as the word "Warning" flashed green on the screen. *Yep, I must've done something wrong, which in this case is right.*

And just to make sure nobody sneaks back in and undoes my good deed for the day . . .

Spider-Man slammed his fist into the top of the console, buckling the metal and sending sparks flying. He ripped the cover off and reached into the mess of wires and transistors inside, tearing them out by the handful until the computer console was reduced to nothing more than a pile of ruined, unrecognizable junk.

That done, Spider-Man turned and headed toward the door. *Now to get tall, green, and ugly and blow this joint before this joint blows!*

But before the Wall-crawler could reach the exit,

the wall in front of him exploded into the room in a
roaring rain of concrete and steel.

"Holy jumpin' . . ."

That was all Spider-Man could get out before he
was buried beneath the collapsing wall.

Chapter 26

THE HULK TUMBLED BACKWARD AS the floor before him erupted in a shower of red-hot concrete chips from the pencil-thin crimson beam that shot from the sky. Foot-wide craters appeared in a straight line along the floor as SpySat, following the orders transmitted to it by Spider-Man, fired after the big green man's rolling body.

The red-hot ray splashed across his legs, singeing his pants and eliciting a roar of agony from the emerald Goliath. The maser beam continued along its path, blasting the debris that covered virtually every foot of the floor with molten slag. It flashed into the deep launch well.

A geyser of flame exploded from the pit as the machine struck pipelines running beneath the steel-plated bottom. An earth-shaking explosion shook the building.

The Hulk lay sprawled on the floor watching the

progress of the flashing maser with an expression of bewilderment on his broad face. He could not understand what was happening anymore. He had done as the bug-eyed man had told him and demolished the big building. So why had the light come back to bother him now?

With a grunt, he climbed to his feet and lumbered across the wreckage-strewn floor, through the wall of flame billowing from the pit, to the other side of the hangar. He shoved petulantly at the debris all around him.

"Nothing left to smash," he grumbled angrily. "Hulk better go look for bug-eyes now. Maybe he can tell Hulk what to smash . . . huh?"

The Hulk hunched over as the maser beam suddenly turned from its path and skimmed across his back. He bellowed in pain and anger and swiped his big green hands futilely at the air. In his blind rage, the man-brute stumbled over a beam from the ceiling and crashed into the one wall still left standing. It cracked in several directions.

He whirled, his back to the wall, in time to see a crimson flash from the sky coming toward him. He threw himself to the floor, the heat of the beam searing across his back and blasting into the weakened wall.

With a thundering roar, the wall collapsed into the next room.

"Holy jumpin' . . ."

The Hulk's head jerked around and his beady eyes narrowed. Had he heard something in the next room . . . ? Somebody had cried out when the wall fell. Somebody whose voice he recognized . . . *bug-eyes!*

The man-monster roared out Spider-Man's name and sprang to his feet and into the chamber revealed by the collapsed wall. His eyes darted about frantically and then he started to heave huge chunks of concrete aside. The blocks flipped through the air and crashed into consoles, through the view screen, and caused small explosions to erupt throughout the room, followed by electrical sparks that fizzled and turned into fires.

After long, agonizing seconds, the Hulk shoved aside a piece of wall and spotted a patch of color beneath the dull-gray concrete. It was bright red.

"Don't worry, bug-eyes," the man-brute breathed heavily as he pushed aside the remaining wreckage. "Hulk will save you, friend."

Finally, the Hulk pulled Spider-Man free of the debris. Gently, he lowered the still youth to the ground and brushed his thick fingers across the Web-slinger's face.

"Bug-eyes?" the Hulk grumbled tentatively.

The jade giant flinched as a powerful explosion shook what remained of the hangar. Startled, he saw the battered consoles erupt into fire and smoke. He lifted Spidey's limp form, cradled him gently in one arm, and bounded from the control room. His escape was cut off by the steady rain of maser blasts bombarding the hangar. He turned to lope around the deadly fire.

"Stop, monster!"

Pendergast stood at the mouth of the long corridor directly across from the Hulk. His elegantly tailored suit was ripped, with one sleeve hanging free and covered with dust and grime. His neatly clipped gray-and-silver hair was in disarray. In his hands was a rifle of some sort, one with a bulky canister clipped to its stock.

"Go away, little man," the Hulk snarled, waving the tall man aside. "Hulk has had enough smashing and fighting today. Now Hulk just wants to be left alone."

"You'll be left alone all right, monster," Pendergast shouted, his steel-gray eyes flashing madly. "You'll be left alone for all of eternity! I'm going to kill you and that damned, interfering insect for what you've done!" His voice broke as he screamed across the room. The explosions taking place somewhere beneath the floor were growing louder and stronger, rocking the hangar. "You've destroyed me," he sobbed. "You've destroyed us all!"

Spider-Man moaned as his eyes flicked open. *Ohhh, my aching back . . . and everything else!* Slowly, he realized he was being held in the Hulk's massive arms. He rapped his knuckles on the big green man's ribs. "Hulk . . ." he muttered.

Without looking at his companion, the Hulk lowered the Wall-crawler to the floor. Spidey tested his legs and saw he could stand.

"Hulk said go away!"

Oh-oh. Sounds like we're not alone!

Spidey saw Pendergast. "You better do as he says, mister," he called, his head still spinning. "He hasn't had his morning coffee yet and he can get real crabby if you bug him."

Pendergast raised his weapon. "He'll never get the chance."

"In case you're forgetting, guns aren't much good against . . ."

"And in case *you're* forgetting, Spider-Man, this gas *is!*" Pendergast started to giggle but caught himself. "And before either of you can get within a dozen feet of me, you'll *both* be unconscious.

"The maser beam and explosions once the fire reaches the fuel-storage tanks will take care of you and Bruce Banner from there!"

Not if we go up, it won't!

"C'mon, Greensleeves. We're splitting!" Spidey whispered.

The Hulk pushed Spider-Man aside, still glowering at Pendergast. "Hulk warned you, little man. Hulk gave you the chance to leave Hulk in peace, but little man would not go." He flexed his mighty leg muscles and sprang toward Pendergast.

Pendergast screamed as a quarter ton of muscle and sinew descended toward him. The tall man swung his weapon up and wildly pulled the trigger.

A thick cloud of gas billowed from the nozzle,

swirling around the Hulk. But the man-monster was prepared for the fumes this time and he had filled his mighty lungs before he leaped. He thumped to the floor and effortlessly plucked the gun from Pendergast's hands. Lifting the tall man over his head, he brought Pendergast's face up to his own, his lips curling in a snarl.

"Hulk warned you!"

The man-brute shook the white-faced man roughly and then, with an animallike cry, flung him to the ground. Pendergast collapsed with a sigh.

The Hulk started to turn and, as he did, the maser beam moved across the floor toward him.

"Watch it, Hulk," Spidey cried, but it was too late. The narrow beam of ruby-red light exploded across the Hulk's chest.

The man-monster gasped in surprise and pain and, in doing so, inhaled large amounts of the noxious gas that still hovered about him. He bellowed in anger, but the cry weakened as the nerve toxin attacked his system. The mighty Hulk began to stagger, his normally dull eyes more glazed over than ever. His arms and legs felt like great weights that he could no longer support. The great green Goliath collapsed to the floor with a strangled groan.

Spider-Man dived from the maser beam's path as it moved past him, back toward the control room. He was back on his feet instantly, running toward the Hulk. *Pendergast said something about rocket fuel . . . and as soon as that beam finds it, it's big-boom-boom time in the old town tonight!*

The Hulk was changing as he lay sprawled across the floor. His great body glowed with green energy and he was shrinking as the gas slowed his heartbeat and respiration. The primitive face relaxed, softened as the features changed to something more closely resembling a man, until, mere moments after the metamorphosis began, Dr. Bruce Banner had reclaimed his mind and body.

Maybe he's no good in a fight this way, but it sure as heck makes him easier to carry outta here!

Spider-Man slung Bruce over his shoulder and, with a final glance at the control room engulfed now in flames and smoke, ran from the hangar into the deserted complex. The sound of trucks and cars was just fading into the distance as Spidey ran toward the Niagara River just down the sloping shore from the hangar.

Bahwhoooom!

Spider-Man felt himself being lifted off the ground and swept through the air by the force of the explosion that followed the maser beam's striking the underground tanks containing highly volatile rocket fuel. The little that the rampaging Hulk had left standing of the once-proud hangar blew straight up into the sky.

Together, Spider-Man and Bruce Banner splashed into the rushing waters of the Niagara River.

23,000 miles in space, SpySat spun faithfully in its orbit with the Earth. Its internal mechanisms operated smoothly and soundlessly in airless space as it flashed its maser beam Earthward.

Then, to put it mildly, the satellite became confused.

Commands ceased being beamed to its computers for several seconds, then new information flowed in. New coordinates were set and the maser swung its aim. Then, just as suddenly, its telemetric links with Earth stopped, a signal for all systems to shut down. Automatically, the lens that beamed the maser Earthward closed its protective cover. But the maser still fired. It took only a few minutes for the internal heat of the satellite to rise dangerously.

SpySat exploded in a brief flash of fire.

But in the vacuum of space there was no sound.

Chapter 27

THE ROAR OF RUSHING WATER FILLED Spider-Man's ears as his head broke the surface of the raging Niagara River.

The current carried the Web-slinger and the still-unconscious Bruce Banner rapidly down the wide river. Spidey struggled to keep the young scientist's head above water.

Hunks of ice ranging in size from that of a base-ball to that of an automobile swirled about them, as Spidey and Banner were carried by the powerful current. Spidey realized it had been more than two days since his capture by Pendergast and his crew, enough time for the unseasonably warm weather to thaw the river and send it flowing along to its ages-old destination:

The falls!

The Wall-crawler realized it with a start and tried paddling desperately for the shore, but the current was too powerful for him to overcome with his unconscious burden. He turned on his back and allowed himself to be swept along as he supported Bruce's limp form against the length of his body.

Panic started to take hold of the Web-slinger and he had to try hard to fight it. He took quick gulps of air and forced himself to be calm. *Be cool, Parker! Panicking will only make sure we get killed, but maybe, just maybe, we have a chance if I can keep calm. . . .*

He took another deep breath. *Okay, okay. I've heard of people going over the falls in barrels or capsules, so I know it's been done before.*

Only thing I don't ever remember hearing is if any of the schmoes who tried it survived!

The pounding of the water roaring over the falls to the rocks far, far below grew louder.

Even if they did, what good does that do me? They would've had time to prepare for it with special equipment, a padded capsule to take the impact of crashing down to those rocks. I've got less than a minute and there's not a barrel in sight.

Whoa! Think again, Web-head!

Spider-Man turned in the water and swam frantically with Bruce toward a large chunk of ice flowing along with them. He strained his battered, weary muscles to the utmost and reached the floe. Grunting with effort, he lifted Bruce out of the water and onto it, following right behind.

The Wall-crawler knelt and began to spin something from his unique chemical webbing. He worked desperately, fashioning a large, thick cocoon big enough to hold two. He glanced up every few seconds to check on their progress along the thundering waterway.

By the time he stood, the makeshift barrel completed, the roar of the falls was deafening. He knew his and Bruce's time was measured in milliseconds now. He lifted Bruce and dropped him into the thick web barrel, following him inside. It was a tight fit, but it would have to do. Spray from the rumbling falls formed a thick, impenetrable mist as Spider-Man webbed closed the top of his barrel.

Then, hugging his knees to his chest, the Web-slinger waited.

The barrel tipped suddenly at a sharp angle and then rolled head over heels as it tumbled over the edge of Niagara Falls.

It was like the worst roller-coaster ride he could imagine and falling from a great height at the same time. The barrel spun madly about, tipping every which way as the pounding waters bounced it back and forth.

Spidey felt his stomach churn and heave sickeningly. He knew had he had any food down there, it would not have stayed down very long after this ride began. Irrationally, he realized it had been over seventy-two hours since he last ate. *Stupid*.

The stomach-wrenching trip seemed to go on forever before the web barrel hit something hard with a jar that sent agony shooting up the Wall-crawler's spine. Bruce Banner, limp and unconscious, seemed no worse off from the trip.

The barrel bounced and spun again before landing with another painful jolt against something hard and unyielding. *The rocks! We're hitting the rocks!*

It went on like that for several more seconds until Spider-Man thought he would scream in pain and then there was a final, gentle jolt and the barrel was bobbing gently upright in the calm water at the bottom of the falls.

Spider-Man exhaled through clenched teeth, realizing that he must have been holding his breath the whole way down. He shook his head and smiled shakily to himself.

Stupid.

"Oh, man," Spidey moaned. "Even my aches have aches."

Bruce Banner huddled before the small fire the

Web-slinger had managed to build after dragging himself and Bruce from the bottom of the falls. Though the day was warm, the half-naked scientist was chilled from his plunge into the icy river. "I must say," the young scientist smiled, "I'm almost sorry I wasn't around for the big event."

"Which one? The complex going up or us going down?"

"Hmm." Bruce shook his head. "Come to think of it, I'm *glad* I missed them both. From what you told me, it sounded pretty bad." He stared into the crackling fire, the smile fading from his handsome face. "Are you sure it's gone?" he asked without looking up.

"The satellite?" Spidey squatted before the fire and held out his gloved hands to be warmed. "I did a pretty thorough number on the controls." He shrugged. "Even if it's not destroyed, there's little chance anybody will be able to get at it. Very few cabbies are willing to go into that neighborhood."

"Then I guess some good came out of this," Bruce said softly.

"What do you mean? What else were you here for?"

The scientist laughed bitterly. "A dream."

"Look around you, Doc. Ain't no dreams around here. Just water."

"The Hulk's some kind of hero in all this, right?" Bruce said into the fire. "He's helped make the world safe for democracy and all that crap, right? Well, can I tell you something you might find hard to swallow, friend? I would have given up today's little victory willingly and let them have their satellite to do with as they pleased to whomever they pleased if there *had* been a cure for me here."

"Hey, c'mon, Doc," Spider-Man said. "It's not all that bad?"

"Isn't it, Spider-Man? I'm a radiation-created freak, a mindless rampaging monster whose sole purpose in life is to destroy," Bruce said sharply. "Suddenly, half my life is no longer my own and the other half is shattered beyond repair by something *I* do but can't remember because it's not even me doing it."

Spidey looked at the taut-faced scientist, silent.

"It's not even a life anymore," Bruce said half aloud. "Sometimes I wonder what horrible thing I could have done to offend God to deserve this."

"Bull!" Spidey exclaimed.

Bruce Banner's head jerked up. "What?"

"I said bull, Doc."

"Look, I appreciate your saving my life and all, Spider-Man, but you don't know what this is all about."

"You'd be surprised, Doc. How do you think I got the way I am? By sending in fifty cents and my Post Toasties box tops? No, friend, I was the lucky sucker who got to be standing there when a radioactive spider decided it had to bite somebody.

"And I've had my share of tragedies, too—like the sweetest old man who ever lived, the wonderful man who raised me as his own son, and got killed because of my indifference. Like a life that's so screwed up because of these powers and the damned responsibility that comes with them that sometimes I wonder if it's worth getting out of this costume and leading it like I was a normal human being.

"Maybe what I've gone through doesn't stack up to turning into a green monster, but there's one thing I know for sure and that's that wallowing in self-pity is the thing that'll drag you down quicker than anything you can feel sorry for yourself about."

Bruce Banner didn't say anything for several minute after the Web-slinger's outburst. He stared into the eerie mask that covered the face of the man called Spider-Man from view. "Yeah," he breathed at last. "Yeah." He stood and shoved his hands into his tattered pockets. "You know, friend," he said, "the longer I'm with you, the more I believe J. Jonah Jameson and the *Daily Bugle* are full of so much stale fertilizer."

"That's putting it daintily."

And speaking of Jonah Jameson, I'll bet he and a lot of other folks in the big city are probably wondering where a certain Peter Parker has been hiding the past couple of days!

Spidey got to his feet and began kicking dirt over the fire. "Well, it's been fun, Doc, but this little arachnid has got to be moving on now."

"Just like the Lone Ranger, huh?" Bruce smiled. "The job done, evil banished from the West, you ride off on your faithful steed Silver."

Spidey laughed. "Something like that, only in my case, they ask *'Why* is that man masked?' " The Webslinger extended his hand and clasped Bruce's. "What about you, Bruce? You making the sunset scene yourself?"

Bruce shook Spider-Man's hand with affection. "If that's where I've got to do my looking, I guess so." He shrugged and smiled. "Hell, what I was looking for wasn't here, so it's *got* to be somewhere else, right?"

"Right." Spidey released the young scientist's hand. "And keep in mind if you're ever in need of help in looking, I'm always available, Doc."

"How can I pass up an offer like that from a superhero who's read my books?" He nodded. "And thank you, Spider-Man." The young scientist turned and walked away, huddled against the winter breeze.

Spider-Man waved to the man. "Good luck, Doc."

Then he turned and walked away in the opposite direction.

Chapter 28

"ALL RIGHT, PETER PARKER, YOU'VE got just three seconds to explain where you've been before I kill you for making me worry that somebody might have killed you!"

The stunning blonde-haired girl stormed up to Peter Parker as he walked from the elevator into the bustling city room of the *Daily Bugle,* the words tumbling from her in a jumbled rush. Peter smiled and reached out his arms to embrace the angry girl.

Cindy Sayers stepped back out of his reach. "Not so fast, buster," she snarled. "I've had guys show up late for dates before, but never by four days without at least a phone call and I want an explanation. Now!"

"Don't I even get a kiss?"

"Not till I get an explanation."

"Then if you will just calm yourself, pretty lady, I will tell you."

Cindy folded her arms across her chest. "I'm waiting."

"Well, you see," Peter said, stepping closer to her. "I was out on this assignment that Jameson sent me on and . . . ah-ha!" He grabbed her around the waist and pulled her to him. Before she could protest, he kissed her.

"Got you," he smiled after they separated.

Cindy smiled back and rested her forehead against his chest. "Oh, Peter," she said softly. "I've been so worried about you I thought I was going to die. Why didn't you call?"

Peter gently stroked her soft hair. "I'm sorry, babe," he said. "I didn't mean to worry anybody, but I was caught up in something up in Niagara Falls and . . ."

"Niagara Falls?" Cindy looked startled. "Isn't that where that place . . . the Institute for Radiation Research, blew up yesterday?"

"Well, yes and no," Peter started.

"And just what the hell is that supposed to mean, you ungrateful little thug?" J. Jonah Jameson thundered, trailing a thick cloud of pungent smoke in his wake as he stalked over to the couple by the elevators. "And where have you been all week? What's the idea of running off and leaving Coswell like that? That idiot couldn't find his hand if it was in his pocket much less get back to New York from New Jersey alone and file an intelligible story!"

"I got sidetracked, Mr. J."

"Sidetracked?"

"To Niagara Falls."

Jameson's eyes widened and he slowly took the soggy cigar butt from his mouth. "*You* were in Niagara Falls, Parker?"

Peter nodded.

"Did you . . . ?"

Peter nodded.

"Well!" Jameson screamed.

"Like I was telling the lady," Peter said. "Spider-Man and the Hulk demolished the place. . . ."

"Are you saying Spider-Man's responsible for the institute blowing up?" Jameson asked, hardly believing his good fortune.

"Um, before you start writing your editorial, Mr. Jameson, I think you ought to know that the IRR wasn't what it claimed to be."

The *Daily Bugle* publisher's craggy face fell and it continued falling as the young photographer related the events that took place in upstate New York.

"What happened to all the people?" Cindy asked when he had finished. "They weren't blown up with the hangar, were they?"

"No. Spider-Man cleared everybody out before he wrecked the controls. They were well clear of the hangar when it blew."

Jameson grabbed Peter's arm and shoved his face into the young photographer's. "Does anybody else know any of this?"

"Only everybody who was there, I imagine."

"You know damned well what I mean, Parker," Jameson yelled. "Do I have an exclusive or don't I?"

"It's all yours, Triple-J," Peter Parker smiled.

Jameson clapped his hands together gleefully, visions of increased circulation dancing through his head. "Robertson!" he bellowed, racing across the crowded city room toward his office.

Peter turned back to Cindy and put his arms around her. "Now, where were we before we were so rudely interrupted?"

Cindy stood on her toes and kissed him. "Right about here, handsome," she growled playfully.

"Down girl! Lemme buy you a cup of coffee."

Cindy Sayers pouted playfully. "I thought you loved me," she said.

"More than my authentic Little Orphan Annie Ovaltine cup even, dear lady."

"Then why're you trying to poison me?"

As they walked across the city room to the coffee machine, Jameson charged out of his office and ran up to Peter, holding out his hand. "I almost forgot, kid," he puffed. "Let me have them."

Peter looked at the outstretched hand and then at Jameson. "Have what, you merciless giver of straight lines?"

"The pictures, stupid!"

"Pictures?"

"You been taking parrot lessons, kid?"

"*What* pictures?"

"The pictures," Jameson said slowly through clenched teeth, his face slowly turning a deep shade of scarlet, "that you damned well better have taken of the Hulk and the blasted Wall-crawler tearing up that Niagara Falls complex."

Peter grinned sheepishly. "Would you believe I . . ."

Jameson held up his hand. "*Don't* say it, Parker, because even *I* wouldn't believe that you're stupid enough to be in the middle of one of the biggest stories of the century and *not* get any photographs."

Peter shrugged. "Sorry about that, chief."

The *Bugle* publisher merely stared in disbelief at his young employee.

"Uh, I think we'd better get out of here real fast, lover," Cindy said softly to Peter. "Any second now, he's going to come out of this stupor and most probably break you into several hundred little bite-size pieces and feed you to the pigeons."

Peter nodded and, together, they hurried back to the elevators and out of the building, leaving J. Jonah Jameson standing in the center of his city room, speechless for one of the rare times in his life.

"Hey, Pete," Cindy said when they were out on the street. "How come you didn't get pictures anyway?"

Peter looked at her, feigning astonishment. "You ought to know better than to ask a question like that, Cindy! I was too busy helping the Hulk."

"What?" she laughed.

"That's right," he said defensively. "Heck, he never would've been able to do what he did without me."

Cindy was still laughing.